KISSING
VANESSA

KISSING
VANESSA

Simon Cheshire

delacorte press

Published by
Delacorte Press
an imprint of
Random House Children's Books
a division of Random House, Inc.
New York

Visit us on the Web! www.randomhouse.com/teens
Educators and librarians, for a variety of teaching tools, visit us at
www.randomhouse.com/teachers

Library of Congress Cataloging-in-Publication Data
Cheshire, Simon.
Kissing Vanessa / Simon Cheshire.
p. cm.
Summary: Fifteen-year-old Kevin has plans to do better in school, but
when the next term begins he is smitten by his new classmate, Vanessa,
and he focuses all of his energy on getting close to her.
ISBN 0-385-73212-0 (trade)—ISBN 0-385-90242-5 (GLB)
[1. Love—Fiction. 2. Schools—Fiction. 3. High schools—Fiction.
4. Interpersonal relations—Fiction. 5. England—Fiction.] I. Title.

PZ7.C425213Ki 2004
[Fic]—dc22
2003062583

The text of this book is set in 10.5-point Arial.

Book design by Kenny Holcomb

Printed in the United States of America

October 2004

10 9 8 7 6 5 4 3 2 1

BVG

To all those I love,
and in memory of Min

PROLOGUE

I will kiss Vanessa Wishart. I will kiss those soft and tender lips. I will prove to her that I love her with all my heart, and with all my soul. This is my solemn vow.

Amen.

ONE

same-old, same-old

So, anyway, it's the first day of the new term, and I'm feeling quietly positive about school for once. I got a couple of projects finished over the holidays, and I think I can look the letters E, X, A and M square in the face again and not shudder with revulsion and fright. This term I'm fifteen, this term I've caught up with work, this term I'm going to fulfill the potential that my school reports keep going ON and ON and ON about.

Just before nine, we're all in assembly. The whole school. Sitting pretty quiet, too. Most of the losers in this place are still suffering from all the excess sleep and daytime telly-watching they clocked up through Easter. Not like me. I, Kevin Watts of 10L, am neat, tidy (new tie!) and alert.

So's Jack, sitting next to me. Alert, I mean. He's spotted a new face filing onto the stage with all the other teachers.

The new teachers are easy to spot. They're the ones who still look like they have a shred of hope left. They gaze out across the scraggy-haired ocean of pupils in front of them with a certain burning defiance in their eyes. You won't get me, Warwick High.

Oh yes, we will. In the end, we get 'em all. It's kind of a badge of honor among us pupils. It's a real achievement to have got the kind of tough reputation we've got, as a student body. It requires years of dedicated misbehavior, through generations of kids. If those teachers could harness the energy we put into subverting everything they do, they'd get us passing postdoctorate degree exams by the age of twelve.

"Whoooo is that?" purrs Jack. He cranes his neck to get a better look at the young female teacher taking a seat in the middle of the modern languages staff.

"Oh, for God's sake," I mumble. "Put it away."

"She's niiiice," says Jack.

"You said that about Mrs. Berridge, and look what a ratbag she turned out to be close up."

"That's no Mrs. Berridge, that's a *fox*," drawls Jack, his eyebrows doing a quick loop-the-loop.

"What is it with you and older women?" I whisper.

"I can't help it if ladies in their twenties respond to my teen-animal magnetism."

"You're sick," I whisper. "You're a sick man."

I have to admire my pal Jack, though. He IS the very essence of self-assurance. And he's got the sort of slightly crumpled, hooded-eyed looks that some girls seem to find magnetic; a carefully maintained personal style that's somewhere between "How yoo doin'?" and "Couldn't give a stuff anyway." He's out on dates every weekend without fail, and a different girl nearly every time, too. He's got it all worked out when it comes to girls. Although you don't have to know him that well to realize that his mind's filthier than the science block toilets.

He cranes his neck the other way, never taking his eyes off Miss Newteacher. His mouth keeps wiggling like he's limbering up for a snog.

Last onto the stage comes Mr. Pewsey, the headmaster. Legend has it that his spirit was finally broken by the school Christmas pageant of 1992. The file in the secretary's office puts his age at forty-seven. He looks well past that. Even Jack feels sorry for him sometimes. Mind you, Mr. Pewsey's got a nasty streak. There's only so far you can push him before he snaps.

Mr. Pewsey shuffles to the lectern, front and center of the stage. The staff, seated in rows behind him, stare glassily at us. We stare back. The kids closest to the stage smile and wave occasionally.

Mr. Pewsey clears his throat. For a few seconds, there is silence. I can almost hear the dusty creak of his shoes and the chalky squeak of the leather patches on his jacket elbows.

"Good morning, everyone," he says quietly.

"Hiya, mate!" pipes up an anonymous silly voice from the twelfth grade.

He ignores it. "I hope you've all had a refreshing and invigorating holiday," he says, very nearly managing a smile. His head nods like a wise tortoise, and the vertical sunlight streaking through the narrow, floor-to-ceiling windows of the hall glints off his glasses. Ah—start of the new term, he's given them a polish. Maybe his spirit isn't entirely broken after all.

He continues flatly: "I know I've had a bundle of laughs." He pauses. Sorry, sir, was that a hilarious one-liner? But the moment passes, and nobody so much as coughs. His shoulders slump. "So . . . welcome back for the spring term. I trust those of you hurtling toward examinations are already beginning your review timetables. If not, the hurtling will hurt you a great deal more than it hurts me . . ."

—cough at the back—

"Before we start the first lesson of the day, there are a couple of notices." He consults the limp sheet of paper in his hand. "The drama club will now meet on Wednesdays instead of Thursdays, because of Mrs. Berridge's hospital appointments; the side entrance to the science block is now out of bounds to all except twelfth graders, following the . . . regrettable incident last term; and we welcome a new member of staff, Miss Monique DuBois, who'll be taking over years eight, nine and ten French classes."

Miss Monique DuBois smiles shyly at the audience. She looks like a cross between a Grecian statue and an Afghan hound.

"*Sacré bleu,*" growls Jack with a grin. "She's French. *La* sexy!"

"Maybe it's just her name that's French," I say.

"What? French name, teaches French, looks French, therefore IS French. Jeez, you've got a lot to learn, Kev."

"I can't be bothered. I'm not getting involved in any of your harebrained schemes this term, Jack. This is the new, dynamic, supercool me."

Mr. Pewsey spreads his arms in a floppy get-lost gesture. "That is all. Fly to your perches, my little magpies of learning."

There's an almighty scraping of chair legs and a collective outpouring of sneezes and chatter. But before I can stand up . . . OH MY GOD! . . . an icy terror suddenly strikes at my heart. Terror, because there's a definite warm, wet feeling soaking through the seat of my trousers.

What . . . ?

Oh my God. Oh my God, I never so much as felt it coming. Oh my God, I'm fifteen and I'm . . .

. . . incontinent?

I jump to my feet. Oh my God, I'm soaked! Holy flippin' Jesus mother of . . .

Giggles over my shoulder. I turn around, and there's whatsisname from 9B, the kid with the hair that'd make a carrot look gray and colorless. And his pencil-thin sidekick, he of the meganose.

"Hiya, Watts!" they chime. "Bit of luck us sitting right behind you, wannit?" Carrot holds up his plastic lemon squeezy.

I put on a hmm-yeah expression. "Warm water. Nice touch. Very realistic."

"Why can't orifices like you two give it a rest, eh?" says Jack. They give him a squirt up the back of the blazer and saunter off.

"Loooosers," they chant, vanishing into the crowd. Jack gives himself an exaggerated Labrador shake and carries himself away on that lolloping, attitude-rich walk of his.

So much for the new term. So much for the new me. Looks like it's the same old manky rubbish as always. Same-old, same-old . . .

TWO

on second thoughts:
not same-old, same-old; in fact, turning
point of my entire life

Half past nine, French. Naturally, by this time I'm staring out of the window. Despite the wad of loo paper stuffed into my pants, the damp patch on my trousers has spread up my zip and is still uncomfortable.

Jack is feeling dejected and upset. Miss Monique DuBois has turned out to have the thickest Glaswegian accent I've ever heard. When she speaks French it sounds like an explosion in a razor-blade factory. Haven't caught a single word of anything she's said yet. Jack is choking back the emotion of the moment.

So I'm sitting by the window, and I'm staring out of it, and I'm wishing I had my camera with me. Outside, across the sports field, there's a shifting circle of light, bright shafts piercing the low clouds. They're moving over the trees next to the main road, and rippling across the field. The effect is weird-looking, sort of unreal. Beautiful. It's exactly the sort of thing you only see once in a blue month of Sundays.

I curse myself that I've left my camera at home. As digital cameras go, it's one of the smaller, slimmer models, but the lens is a pretty good spec. Not top-of-the-range, optics-wise, but I wanted something compact enough to keep in my pocket. So I guess you have to make compromises. Only . . . of course . . . today . . . it's on my desk at home.

I let out a sigh. The shafts of light have gone, fading out of existence as the clouds shift and let the sun get a look-in. That would have made a fabulous shot. I can already think of a place for it, once I'd got it printed out: framed next to my shot of the frosted tree I caught in January, which I insisted went in the living room at home.

Everyone's got a kind of half-frown. If you were being generous you'd say it was the deep concentration of eager, dedicated students. If you weren't being generous you'd say we were all just trying to make out what the hell Miss Monique DuBois is talking about. Still, credit where credit's due: it's got us very quiet and attentive. Well, attentive except for me, really.

No! Wrong attitude! There's a new me this term, right? No daydreaming, no drifting off the point, no framing terrifically atmospheric photos in the middle of French. It's a GOOD thing I've forgotten my camera.

I sigh again. Quietly. I don't want to distract the rest of the class from their frowning.

I notice that Kate Stumpage has had a stylishly radical haircut during the holidays. Unfortunately, it doesn't suit her pointy-chipmunk face. I saw her parents once at a school fête. They're both pointy-chipmunk too. Poor girl never stood a chance. I mean, she's a nice person. A bit out of focus from the rest of the world, but a nice person. She has a genuinely impressive memory for interesting trivia, and she IS attractive, at least in a way that makes Jack go all smiles and eyebrows . . . I'm not trying to be nasty, or anything. She just looks pointy-chipmunk, that's all.

James is frowning hardest of all of us. It's not that he's hard of hearing, he's just a bit dim. I'm not trying to be nasty again, he IS dim. If someone calls out "Oi, James!" he's right there, but call out "Jimmy!" or "Jimbo!" and he's blank as a new jotter pad. He just isn't the sharpest knife in the drawer, that's all. Jack likes to sit well away from him, because James is officially the Boy All Girls Want to Get Stuck in a Lift With. He looks like a male model. I don't really see it myself—to me, his features look too small to fit properly onto his face. They're too spaced out. But he's captain of the school rugby team too, so that's an added bonus with the girls. Apparently.

There's a tap on my shoulder. Oh Gawd, Gregory Timms.

"Kevin, mate," he whispers. I don't know why, but it really annoys me when people call me that. "Kev . . . Kev, mate . . ."

I lean back slightly. Turning round would attract too much attention. "What?"

"Do you want to come round to my house and zap things on my GameCube? After school?"

Oh, blimey. "Sorry, Gregory. Busy. Thanks, though."

"I've got a new train set," he hisses. I don't need to turn around to know he's grinning like a psychopath.

"Oooh, really tempting," I say. "But I'm busy. Thanks, honestly, thanks, but I can't."

"My mum says she's going to make a cake for tea," he whispers.

"I'm on a strict diet. For health reasons. Sorry."

"I didn't know that," says Gregory, sounding slightly alarmed. "Are you OK?"

Oh, hell's teeth, shut up. People are looking.

"I'm fine," I whisper. "Just mustn't eat icing."

I lean forward and pretend to be listening intently to a sentence about *"la pâtisserie,"* which sounds like *"Ger vinga plaocen le zornki."* Gregory Timms retreats and I catch a glimpse of him biting his lip and wiping his nose on his fingers.

I liked him a lot when we were in the Kindergarten class at PRIMARY school together. But now . . . Do you ever get the feeling that there are some things you just can't escape? I have enough trouble being labeled: Mr. Background, Mr. Daydream and other assorted children's characters, without having anoraks like Gregory Timms in tow. Holy cow, the new me is never going to blossom at this rate!

10:33 a.m.

My eyes casually graze the clock on the wall. But it's like fate. As if time itself is telling me to take note of the exact moment.

10:33 a.m. Now.

Why? Because then it happens.

Then my life changes.

The door creaks open and in shuffles Mr. Pewsey. He's chewing on one of his nerve pills and washing it down with quick sips from a tiny carton of blackcurrant juice. Miss Monique DuBois halts (whether in midsentence or not, nobody can say) and smiles at him.

"My abject apologies for the disturbance, Miss DuBois," he says flatly, dabbing a hand to his forehead. He casts a watery eye over us all for a moment and puts out a hand. "Oh, please don't get up, Ten L."

We just sit there waiting.

"Miss DuBois, I have your new pupil. Ten L, this is Vanessa Wishart, who will be joining your class. I'm sure I can count on you all to greet her with your unique blend of enthusiasm. Vanessa, there's a desk free over there next to Kevin Watts . . . er, the fair-haired boy with the glasses. Kevin, you're a moderately sensible young man. Take Vanessa under your wing for today, will you? Show her the ropes, the toilets, that sort of thing."

He shuffles to one side. I finally get a clear look at Vanessa.

She steps forward, obviously conscious of the sudden silence, her shoes clumping on the floorboards, walking toward the empty desk next to me. She seems nervous, but doesn't look down. She seems to feel us watching her, but doesn't falter, striding along the gap beside the radiator.

She is tall. Her legs are long, her arms slender. Smooth, tapering fingers grip the handle of her bag. She is slim, almost delicate-looking. Straight hair brushes around her neck, the blackest black that hair can be. Her face is pale, sculptured. Elegant, curving lips; a perfect, triangular nose.

And her eyes. Sharp, bright, feline. Spectacular eyes, a vivid, marbled green. Wonderful eyes. She looks at me, into me, through me. Getting closer to me. Her every motion is poise and contour and smoothness.

The bell goes. Kids start moving all around me.

Vanessa is next to me. She flashes me a smile. "Hi. Kevin, is it?"

I appear to stand without using any of the muscles in my legs. I try to speak, I try to tell her that she is the most beautiful girl that I have ever seen, that I will ever see, that has ever existed in all the world.

"Ye . . . Y . . . I . . . Ye-um . . ." I think I may be dribbling.

"Are you OK?" she says.

"He's on a special diet," says Gregory Timms, marching past.

"I'm . . . H'lo, I'm Kevin," I stammer. "So . . . I . . . I'm to show you the ropes and the toilets, that sort of thing."

Something has caught her attention. She's looking at my trousers. The wet patch is drier, but still visible. The wad of loo paper is forming a lump between my legs.

"Should we start with the toilets, then?" she says, deadpan.

"Oh! No . . . er, this is . . . no, this was . . . umm, done in assembly."

"This school must have some really exciting assemblies," she says, even more deadpan.

Suddenly, I see Jack over her shoulder. He gives me a thumbs-up and indicates his reaction to Vanessa in a way which is both clear and graphic. Then he hops over and shoves me aside.

"Hi, babe," he says. "My name's Jack. Yours must be Gorgeous."

Several other boys are hanging around us too. My mind goes sort of blank and mushy, and before I know what's going on she's been whirled away amid offers to carry her bag and do her homework. I wish I'd said something more intelligent.

But it changes nothing.

Because I know that I love her.

Completely and totally.

Forever and ever.

Amen.

THREE

total perfection

"Yes, I suppose she's very pretty," says Kate Stumpage. Her head makes a sort of curly tilt to one side and her big eyes start blinking like they're doing Morse code.

"She's *phwooar*," says Jack under his breath. Then he shovels in another mouthful of chips. Kate gives him a sneery look. "But not as *phwooar* as you, o'course," he says hurriedly.

"In your dreams," says Kate, making a point of looking the other way.

It's lunchtime and I'm trying to keep an eye out for Vanessa. After all, she's supposed to be under my wing today, officially, and orders are orders. Where would the school be without proper discipline? Where is she? She was behind me in the queue. I got distracted for a moment when Fat Lunch Lady nearly missed my plate with a spoon-splat of mashed potato. Then Thin Lunch Lady's there at the till demanding money with misery and before I know it Vanessa's somewhere over by the fruit.

I spot her. She's just paid and is halfway to me when James and a couple of his rugby-team cronies start talking to her. I'm not sure if the whimper I let out is just inside my head or audible on the outside as well.

"Yes, I suppose she's very pretty," says Kate again. I think she's trying to get my attention.

"Mmm, yes," I say, trying to appear casual.

"Of course, beauty is only skin-deep, and all that," says Kate. "You really have to know someone a long time before you can say they're genuinely beautiful. Don't you think?"

"I think it's only ugly people who ever say that," says Jack. He stabs up a neat stack of chips with his fork. "Present company excepted."

"Oh, eat your chips," says Kate. "Don't you think, Kev?"

"Hmm?" I say. "Er, yeah."

What the hell is James saying to Vanessa? The boy can hardly construct a coherent sentence! She's laughing! Laughing! He's being funny, for God's sake! No, it's OK, she's moving off. She's coming over.

Kate turns to me and gets all strangely urgent. Her hands are doing that twisty dance they do when she starts explaining anything. "It's the long-term that counts in relationships, isn't it? You know, like going through things together. Hard times, you know. Like school."

17

I don't know what the hell she's babbling on about. Vanessa's here. Sit next to me! Sit next to me! Sit next to me!

She sits next to Kate. I notice she's had the same as me, pie and mash. Fantastic, she's not one of the rabbit-food brigade! Kate flares a nostril and chomps at her lettucey salad with a sort of yeah-right look on her face; she's one of those fad-diet sheep who think beauty comes from carbohydrate deprivation.

All morning I've been planning my lunch-break chat. Expertly selected questions to deliver maximum information. I've already sussed that Vanessa is a woman of sensible outlook and intellectual temperament, not unlike myself. She's asked some cracking questions in English. Confidently, you know, hand straight up, words spoken clearly and in precisely the right order. And best of all, she's not one of those ghastly girls who whips down six pages of notes before a teacher's got past "Settle DOWN, Ten L. Can we start, PLEASE."

OK, question one: previous educational experience.

"How are lessons here compared to your last school, Vanessa?" I venture. Good start, straight out, nice vocal tone.

"Fine," she says with a smile. SMILE! AT ME! "I was worried that I'd feel really lost. I thought either you'd have covered stuff I haven't, or vice versa. But I think we're pretty much on a level."

Vice versa! Use of a Latin adverbial phrase! What class!

"I can only apologize for the poor quality of the teaching staff," I say, neatly cutting my pie in two.

"They seem OK," says Vanessa, shrugging. "Although I

have no idea what that French teacher—what's her name?—was going on about? The cross-channel ferry?"

"*La pâtisserie*?" I say helpfully.

Kate quickly starts leafing through her copious worksheets from the French lesson, but by the time she finds a definitive answer we've moved on. She tries to take over the conversation with interesting trivia about crime statistics, but I won't be overtaken.

Question two: previous educational experience, supplementary geographical inquiry.

"Where was your last school?" I say politely, neatly cutting my two bits of pie into four.

"London," says Vanessa, but she's started looking distracted.

Cosmopolitan, too! And well spoken, no trace of a Cockney accent! What's she looking at?

I follow her gaze. Fat Lunch Lady has dolloped mashed potato onto Mr. Pewsey's shoes. Mr. Pewsey's standing there looking at it like it's a dog turd. Fat Lunch Lady's telling Thin Lunch Lady to fetch the mop.

Perfectly normal canteen scene. But then . . .

I turn back from watching Thin Lunch Lady run a dripping mop over Mr. Pewsey's suedes, ready for the usual kind of comments. And there's Vanessa.

A camera in her hand. Pulled from her top pocket. Different make but same size as mine. With a smoothness of finger movements that you only get when you're used to working something without even thinking, she captures Pewsey standing there, with everyone watching him watching his shoes getting wet.

Now I KNOW Vanessa is the perfect woman for me. I know it with a certainty that is unshakable, unquestionable.

She sees me gazing at her. For the first time ever, she lets out a hint of embarrassment. "Sorry," she grins. "Hobby."

Oh, heaven.

Oh, joy.

FOUR

perfect is as perfect does

Oh, rapture.

I arrive home I know not how. I wander lonely as a cloud, that floats on high o'er the bypass. My soul doth sing of soppy stuff.

My house is background, not unlike my social standing. It's the middle Victorian terraced house in a long straight row of identical Victorian terraced houses. Some of the neighbors have painted their window ledges in bright colors here and there, and others have tried to outdo each other with the size of their satellite dishes, but mainly the inhabitants of Albert Street accept things the way they are. You ain't going to stand out in Albert Street.

But what do I care? My heart is packed with high-velocity adoration, and all's right with the world.

When I get in, I sling my bag onto the coat hooks. Whoa! Hooked first time! Am I smokin' or what? Dance through the hall to the funky rhythm in my head, and into the kitchen.

"Hi, Mum."

Mum's stirring a bowl of cake mix with one hand and turning a page in *Boys: Parent-Child Dynamics* with the other. She says she reads that kind of thing because eventually she wants to work in nursery schools. She actually reads that kind of thing to try to make sense of me, and thinks I don't realize. She's wearing the horrible, frilly apron she bought off the market; the words "Yo dis my food, I smack yo face" are printed across her front. There's a streak of flour in her hair.

"Hallo, Kevin," she says brightly. (Warm greeting: *Good Practice in Childcare,* chapter six.) "Have you washed your hands?" (Article: "Deadly Bugs in Our Schools," *Woman's Monthly,* issue 234.)

I keep on dancin'. I snap my fingers and give her a wink. "What's for tea, Mum?"

"Do you want fish fingers or beans on toast?"

Hmm, what would Vanessa have? What tender morsels would pass those perfect lips? We have the same sort of lips, me and her, I reckon. They'd fit together so well. Lips are the windows of the soul, they say. . . . No, that's eyes. . . . We have the same sort of eyes, me and her, I reckon. Well, we've both got two of them.

"Or beefburgers?" says Mum. "Kevin?"

I shimmy past the fridge. "Don't mind. Beans!"

"OK," says Mum. ". . . Or there's fish fingers."

"Umm, no. I'll have beans."

"We've got plenty of fish fingers."

"OK, I'll have fish fingers."

"No, that's fine, beans is fine."

"No, really, Mum. I'll have the fish fingers."

"But you wanted beans."

"Then why go on about fish fingers?"

"Because I don't know which you want. It's up to you."

"OK, I'll have beans!"

"Not fish fingers?"

"Oh, let's just have bloody fish fingers and have done with it!"

She gets out the fish fingers. I slump into the living room. Silly woman's spoilt the moment now.

Hey, Dad's home early! He's in his armchair by the window, from which you can see across the street and down the road to the kiddies' playground. His arms are crossed and his head's lolling forward at a steep angle. The snoring's not too bad at the moment. I think the steep angle's keeping his throat too squashed to let out the really huge noises.

Dad's a gas fitter. I'm not entirely clear on what gas fitters do.

We have beefburgers. Mum gives us a long explanation about why it's not fish fingers, but Dad doesn't really care, he's just eating the things, and frankly I'm too busy thinking about Vanessa to pay much attention.

It never ceases to amaze me that someone like me is the product of someone like them. Of course, I've made all the usual investigations about whether I was actually an

23

adopted foundling, but to my surprise and shock it turns out that these two are my real biological parents after all. Still, I suppose it makes sense that one small, dark person (Mum) and one chunky, blond person (Dad) should give rise to a bloke as strictly average-everything-smack-in-the-middle as I am.

Not like Vanessa, of course. What demigods could have fashioned such a face, such a figure, such a smile?

I bless the DNA of her forefathers for combining so brilliantly.

FIVE

that's me out of the picture, then

The next morning, I find out a lot more about where that wonderful genetic structure came from. And, at that point, I begin to wish that her forefathers hadn't been quite so brilliant after all.

Overnight, the school's grapevine has been putting out branches faster than a mobile phone retail chain. The Warwick High gossip network is the sort of intrusive organization that would make the CIA look seriously out of touch, and when I arrive in class—a few minutes before Vanessa—Kate debriefs me on the latest bulletins.

Quick summary: Vanessa Wishart is the daughter of

Lionel Wishart, "you know, the famous writer." Never heard of him personally, but the words "famous" and "writer" are enough to send shock waves through my spinal column. "Famous" and "writer" don't compare well to "nobody" and "gas fitter," do they? Cue one huge socially embarrassing gap. Think of it: her dad and my dad, chatting amiably over a cocktail at a fashionable party. Wahh! What's wrong with this picture?

It gets worse still: Vanessa Wishart is the daughter of Valerie Parkes, "you know, the famous actress." Now, Valerie Parkes I've heard of. Everyone and his dog's heard of Valerie Parkes. I mean, she's not A-list Hollywood, but they say she's now amassed so many awards for various stage and TV dramas that she's put a shelf in her bathroom to handle the overspill from the living room! It's only a matter of time before they stick the word "Dame" in front of her name.

It gets worse still: their daughter appears to have inherited a fair measure of their artistic talent. Her photography ("Sorry. Hobby," ye gods!) won her prizes in public exhibitions when they lived in London. OK, I'm rather nifty with a camera, even though I say so myself, but holy moley . . . Half the time I rely on leaving the autoexposure switched on, and mostly people aren't terribly interested in even looking at my pictures, let alone pinning rosettes on them!

The Wisharts have moved out of London to find a quieter lifestyle, apparently. To give their daughter a more "ordinary" life and to keep her out of the media spotlight now that she's growing up, apparently. To be in a more convenient location for the string of blockbuster successes that mum Valerie Parkes will soon be enjoying at Stratford-Upon-Avon. Apparently.

"Really?" I say, quietly, as if I somehow expect Kate to say "Naaah! Fooled you!"

"Of course, really," says Kate. "The girl's practically a celebrity."

Kate speaks with more than a hint of bitterness in her voice. Perhaps she's picking up my oh-my-God-noooo vibe. Oh no, it must be obvious. I must look shaken and upset. Blast Kate's innate sensitivity to the wounded and helpless! She tries to cheer up the mood with interesting trivia about high-performance cars, but I can't be bothered. I try to hide my feelings as best I can, and put on a brave face.

I don't manage it very well. For some hideous reason, my mind flashes back to that awful Christmas concert at primary school. For a second, I feel just like I did on the morning of the concert, terrified to go into school, not wanting to stand up in front of everyone and sing. For a second, I can see my mum kneeling down in front of me, buttoning up my coat, drying my tears, telling me to put on a brave face.

I don't stand a chance, do I? Not a chance. Not with a girl like Vanessa.

At that moment, she arrives and strolls in her cool and confident way to her desk. She doesn't see me. She's too cool and confident. She opens her bag and pulls out a couple of workbooks. One or two of the trendier girls start talking to her. Then one or two of the trendier boys, including James. She smiles at them. She still hasn't seen me. Cool and confident.

What was I thinking?

"Hi, Vanessa."

"Hallo, Kevin," she says. "Sorry, didn't see you there. . . . Are you OK?"

"Oh yeah, great, fine, no problem," I lie, lie, lie. "Listen, er, you know we were talking about photography yesterday . . . lunchtime . . ."

"Yes?" She looks at me and I melt. My heart dissolves in the warm glow of her wonderful, wonderful eyes. Bright, marbled green eyes. Feline eyes. Spectacular eyes.

"Well, I—I was just wondering if . . . ," I stammer.

Wondering if what? Eh? Wondering if what? If she'd like to come over and see my photos? Flick through the originals on my iMac screen? See how I've artfully Photoshopped them to bring out the colors? See MY room, in MY house, meet MY parents . . . in MY house?

I don't think so.

Wondering if I could bring some of my photos in to show you? To try to impress you with? Like a toddler showing his new friend his favorite toys? Impress you, when your efforts win prizes?

I don't think so.

"Kevin?" she says.

"I was just wondering . . ." Oh, craaaaap. "I mean, we could do it again sometime. Talk . . . about photography . . . and stuff."

She smiles at me. Her lips part. Perfect, even teeth, the thinnest of gaps between the front two. Her smile halts my grinding nerves, steadies my reeling brain, dries my would-be tears.

She's about to speak, but the Trendy Brigade cut in and start inviting her to parties. She gets distracted.

I don't stand a chance.

SIX

torture! torment! pain!

I talk to her here and there. A minute here. Thirty-five seconds there. Between lessons, or like ships that pass in the lunch queue. But she's never alone. There's never any moment when she's not someone's focus of attention.

"Plenty more birds in the sea, Kev," says Jack. We're slouching on the wall next to the art block, Monday lunch break. Feeling alone, I've reluctantly confessed my inner pain. Jack's nearly stopped giggling.

Then he gives me a highly detailed analysis of his date with Stella from 11G. He claims that she deserves to get a dubious reputation. I groan, mostly to show the theatrical jealousy that you're supposed to show at moments like this. I'm silently impressed, because it's usually the timid girls who seem to like him most, the ones who see a streak of parent-baiting rebellion in him. Stella's got a mouth like a loudspeaker at a rock concert.

She happens to pass by a couple of minutes later and gives Jack a look that Jack says means "Hiya, stud" but that doesn't seem like that to me—in fact, I can't interpret it at all. I'll never understand girls like he does.

Most independent observers attribute Jack's abilities to his upbringing. Being in a house with just his mum and his four older sisters all his life has given him a unique perspective. His carefully honed, what-you-looking-at? exterior has melded with an inner instinct forged by his environment. Like if you were raised in the jungle by wolves, you'd be one seriously scary wolf-boy. Something like that.

Stella from 11G walks away, slowly shaking her head.

"What have you got that I haven't?" I say, close to a sob.

"Listen, Kev, I can't help it if I'm a babe magnet, now, can I?" says Jack. He scratches the back of his tangled hair. There's something about the guy that makes you think he's dragging on a ciggie all the time. (I mean, he doesn't—he's asthmatic—he just kind of LOOKS like he does.) "Some of us have got raw animal pulling power, Kev, me old pal. And some of us haven't. Like you haven't. No offense."

"None taken," I say quietly.

"Look, tell you what, I'll set my charisma to 'low' when I'm around Vanessa. Leave the field more open for you, eh? Can't say fairer than that."

"Thanks."

"Course, most of the rest of the school would have to do the same . . . ," he adds quietly.

"Thanks."

Maybe he's right. Maybe I'm just supposed to wait for Miss Background to come along, and assume she's my ideal match.

Vanessa isn't Miss Background. Vanessa is Miss Shining-Front-of-Stage-Center-Spotlight-Glowing-Fabulous.

I watch her march through every day. I love her ability. I love the way she snaps an acid comment back at anyone who deserves it. I love the neatness of her pencil case. I love the subtlety with which she asks awkward questions during physics.

And the way she . . .

NO! NO! NO!

Stop it! I tell myself. This is torture! I can't go on like this, pining away like a lost puppy dog. I have to accept the situation as it is.

She's gorgeous, she's intelligent, she's talented, sure. Fine. End of story. Go about your business, I tell myself, and focus on more attainable goals. I said I was going to be top of the class with my schoolwork this term, didn't I? New me and all that? Right, well, it's time to focus on that.

And only that.

Right.

I struggle valiantly for days. Days and days. But, in the end, the pain's too much. I can't stop pining like a lost puppy dog. I can't CONCENTRATE.

Homework timetables start to drift. I start finding myself hearing the end-of-lesson bell go and then realizing I can't remember anything since the start-of-lesson bell. I know I've always been solid B-grade material, but at least I was doing my best. Mostly. Now I'm stockpiling Cs and Ds as if there were about to be an alphabet shortage.

I stop eating. Mum gets into more of an oh-my-God-stay-calm panic with every passing teatime.

"Are you feeling all right, Kevin?" Slight tremor in the voice. I absolutely KNOW she's got the number of the hospital pinned up on her little corkboard in the kitchen.

"I'm fine."

"You don't look fine. Have you got a headache?"

"No."

"Or a tummyache?"

"No."

"Or any sort of ache?"

Only heartache. God only knows what horrors she'd resort to if I told her the truth. "No, Mum, I'm fine."

"Then why aren't you eating properly?"

"I'm not hungry."

"You must be hungry. If you're not hungry, you must be ill."

"Man cannot live by bread alone," I say wistfully.

She gives me a funny look. "Do you want a sandwich?"

And so it goes on. Day after day after day. Drip, drip, drip, water torture with Vanessa as the water and . . . no, that doesn't work . . . with my limbs broken on the rack of her love . . . no, that's . . .

AAARGGGHH!

Torture. Pure, utter torture. Like I said. There she is, every day, in almost every class. Sometimes she's sitting very close to me. Sometimes she's sitting on the other side of the room. And always it's like there's only her in the room.

She's all I can think about, wonder about, dream about. This goddess with whom I only get to exchange three sentences at a time. To whom I want to say "I love you" and "I adore you" and "You're the most perfect woman in the world." To whom I actually say "Hi" and "See ya" and "Yawn, yawn, Monday again, ho hum."

For a while, I can tell myself that it's just infatuation. After all, she's one hell of a looker, as Jack would put it. I'm just . . . besotted. I don't love her, I just . . . fancy her. That's it, it's just an unfortunate, advanced case of fancying. Which I will get over. Definitely.

Sure, we have a hobby in common, but lots of people take photos, don't they? Sure, it doesn't take much to see that she's got a brain and a personality that rival her face for sheer gobsmacking ethereal beauty. But . . . so have lots of girls. Lots and lots of girls. Plenty more fish in the harem, as Jack always says.

Get over it. Get over her.

Maybe I can manage it, in time. Given enough school-work to occupy my mind, and enough cold baths and cross-country runs to deaden the stings of fancying.

Then comes the art project. "Perceptions of My World," Mr. Blatt entitles it. Soppy old fool. If there's a weedy angle to be taken on any art topic, Mr. Blatt will take it. The man's about ninety; they only keep him on because they can't find a replacement head of art. He walks around as if the pull of gravity on him is thirty times as strong as it is on the rest of us. Word has it that his favorite pastime is pressing wildflowers. It's no wonder this school's got a lousy reputation for artistic achievement.

Anyway, everyone in my class spends a week doing

paintings of their house, or collages of their pet hamster, and having a thoroughly miserable time. "The best three projects will be exhibited in the main hall," says the soppy old fool. Gee whiz, there's an incentive! Come on, gang, let's get out the crepe paper!

Kate Stumpage does pencil drawings of her family. And does them well, I think, or at least accurately, because the whole Stumpage clan seems to share her pointy-chipmunk appearance and drifty off-centeredness. Although if her gran really does look like that she deserves a medal for having the bravery to leave the house. There are some minds you can fathom, and some you can't, and penciled there are half a dozen minds who are clearly in a world of their own.

Gregory Timms does this very long painting of his train set. He tells me he's painted me into carriage two, row three. I thank him through gritted teeth and run away.

James misreads Mr. Blatt's title and goes around town with a video camera capturing reception desks. Mr. Blatt thinks it's a brilliantly clever comment on modern society and instantly puts the film into the final three.

With my emotions drained dry, the best I can manage is a collection of my recent photos. I include the rosy, soft-focus ones I did of my cousin's new baby, which made the parents cry with joy. They end up having much the same effect on Mr. Blatt. Also included are some shots of me, Mum and Dad smiling happily at the local funfair last year. The smiles are meant as an ironic juxtaposition to my present state of mind. Mr. Blatt doesn't spot that one.

Vanessa's project—six 8 x 10 photos—also makes the final three. I've deliberately kept my sorry effort out of her way, but equally I haven't seen anything of her project until I see it exhibited with the others in the lobby on the way into the main hall a few days later.

They're the sort of images I'd never have thought to capture in a million years. They're all in black and white, very stark and bold. At first I pull a face inside my head and think they're a bit harsh, but then I look at them properly and they kind of lead me toward them. I just wouldn't know where to start if someone told me to go out and copy their style, but as I look at them they MEAN something.

There's one of a street; she must have had to squat down in the middle of the road to take it. It's perfectly symmetrical, trees on one side, trees on the other, houses at regular intervals into the distance, cars parked exactly on opposite sides of the road.

There's another she's taken of herself, in a bathroom mirror. You can see the camera held up in front of her nose— her eyes are peeping over the top, eyebrows raised. You can't see her mouth but you can tell she's putting on a cheeky grin. She's slightly to one side of center, low down in the frame. The edges of the mirror frame her, and in the mirror you can see behind her the frame of a doorway, and beyond that another doorway across a hall, and beyond that a tall cupboard, all of them marking out the picture in straight, rectangular lines. Except for Vanessa. And her cheeky grin.

Another of the pictures is of a man at a desk. He obviously doesn't know he's being photographed. She's shown him intent on what he's doing, typing at a PC, but at the same time she's made him look sort of distant, kind of a long way away even though he takes up most of the picture.

There's a photo of a garden in winter, with icicles and a robin. And one of a bedroom that's perfectly neat and tidy except for the wardrobe, with open doors, crammed full of stuff from bottom to top. And one of a line of books on a shelf, that you can't help tilting your head to read the titles of.

They're beautiful. And somehow a bit sad. I look at those photos and I love her more than ever before. I can see into her head, and it's just like looking into mine. Only . . . from a different angle.

Oh, boy.

If it was torture before, it's double torture now. Triple torture! It's like those added layers of chocolate they keep putting into things: New Flavor! Limited Edition! Quadruple Multi-Thick Choco-Extra! You Know You Want It!

This is where I start going slightly peculiar. Of course, I've always carried my camera around with me as a matter of habit, but now it's never out of my hand. At the slightest excuse I start snapping away. What sort of excuse? Vanessa's standing somewhere in front of me, that's what sort of excuse! Often she waves or pulls a face straight into the lens.

Pretty soon I've amassed what can only be called . . . a collection. Oh, dear God, I've gone STRANGE! The only thing that stops people commenting about it all at school is that I've always taken loads of pictures around the place. Plus, of course, Vanessa's always on the lookout for an interesting pic too.

What if somebody notices? What if someone sees I'm going snap-happy? Worse, what if they spot who it is who ends up getting snapped most of the time? I start taking random shots of buildings, to throw casual observers off the scent.

I am a hopeless basket case. I'm still staring at her in class, for God's sake! Sideways as much as possible, so nobody realizes, until my eyeballs hurt, but staring all the same. Once or twice she turns and spots me and I make her jump. Oh God, now I'm FRIGHTENING and strange.

And, all the time, days whizz past in a blur and I get home, go to start my homework and realize I've not listened to a word in class all day.

It's no good. I need help. I need Jack.

SEVEN

the obi-wan of warwick high

Jack flops himself down on his bed and puts his hands behind his head. I hover by the window nervously, looking out at his mum, who's savagely digging the flower borders in their garden.

"Does anyone else know about this?" says Jack.

I shake my head emphatically. Jack nods wisely.

Jack's room is quite possibly the single untidiest place I've ever been in. And I've seen the staff room on a Friday afternoon. I'm hovering by the window partly because of the decimated state of my entire nervous system, and partly because the only surfaces you could sit on are covered with clothes, towels, deodorants, tubes of stuff to gel your hair, tubes of stuff to ungel your hair, and enough brands of aftershave to open the Aftershave Museum and still have plenty over to run a branch of Just Aftershave. Jack is adamant that it's NOT untidy, it's just organized how HE likes it and that this way he knows where everything is.

His mum and his sisters generally avoid coming in here. I'm reliably informed that his eldest sister left home for a week because the fog of grooming-product smells that floats around the upper floor of the house started taking the shine off her jewelry. His mum keeps opening his window when he's not at home, and she attacks the place with assorted fog-absorbing substances from time to time, but there's an atmosphere of TV-ad locker rooms that seems to have seeped into the very walls and is impossible to erase. Maybe that's why I like Jack so much: there's a sense of permanence about him. A fixed point in a shifting world. He's always held the view that his aftershave archive will be a valuable resource to bequeath to his grandchildren one day. It's just that everyone has to step over it at the moment.

His male colleagues at school, those who follow his teachings in the ways of love, say that he lives in an untidy environment because he's focused. He's on a mission, as it were, and he can't afford to be distracted. Which makes sense, doesn't it? And they do say that genius and eccentricity go hand in hand.

I try not to tread on any of the aerosol cans that are lined up around my feet. I ask if I can clear a space to kneel in, but he says he's got all the cans along that wall in strict alphabetical order and I'm not to disturb them.

"I'm glad you haven't gone blabbing to the whole world

about your little problem, Kev," he says. "It doesn't do to have women know you've gone totally soppy over them."

"Doesn't it?"

"No," he says, pointing with both hands for emphasis.

"Don't they think it's romantic?"

"No." He sits up, shaking his head. He pauses, choosing his words carefully. "Kev, Kev, Kev . . . You have so much to learn, oh, my faithful apostle."

He pauses, with a not-quite-sure look on his face. I think his mind must eventually be made up by the pleading, desperate expression I've taken to wearing these days.

Finally, he says, "I'm going to show you something, Kev."

My mind does a sudden recoil. Noticing what he's added in marker pen to the posters of various female pop stars on his walls, this could mean anything.

He ferrets about under his bed for a moment and pulls out a chunky pad, stuffed with odd bits of paper. "Now, as you know, Kev, I've achieved something of a reputation at school. Kids, especially the inexperienced ones like you—no offense, Kev—"

I raise a hand. None taken.

"—often come to me and ask the sort of questions you're asking me. How can I attract girls? Et cetera and so forth. And if they seem worthy, then I tell them. The way I look at it, I got a gift, and it's only fair of me to share it with the world."

"You're a generous guy, Jack," I say, with the heaviest weight of sarcasm I can manage to hold up.

"Right," he says, pointing his finger like a gun. "So, not long ago, I get to thinking to myself, Jack, why not write it all down? Why not condense your wisdom into words? And this is the result. It's not finished yet, not by a looong way, but it's a work in progress."

He holds up the front of the pad. On it is the title of his masterwork, *Girlfriend Management the Easy Way.* For a moment, I stare in disbelief. Jack is planning on being a self-help guru?

"Holy crap, Jack," I say at last. "You're gonna be rich."

"That's what I figure," says Jack. "But all in good time. The important thing is to get it complete. Watertight. Fool-proof."

"Right! Right!" I agree wholeheartedly, nodding like mad. I mean, what the hell, if anyone can be a self-help guru, surely it's Jack? He knows his subject, he's a persuasive communicator and his people-organizing skills are second to none. He talked Stella of 11G into a date, didn't he?

"The way I look at it is this, Kev. I allow you selected— SELECTED—access to this manuscript, under my close personal supervision. In return, I document your use of my methods, and use them as a case study to add into lesson nine. What d'ya say?"

"I say 'thank you,' " I say, grinning.

"The case study will be anonymous, of course," he says.

"Sure."

"I mean, when young men the world over are consulting my book on a daily basis, you don't want them knowing it's you who's the one labeled Pathetic Lovesick Hound of War-wick High, do you?"

"Er, no."

He hands me the pad. I take it with trembling hands and

flick through the first couple of sheets. The contents page is enough to give me a firm sense of reassurance. There's a science in Jack's approach that you simply can't deny:

Lesson One: *Attracting Girls Isn't as Hard as You Think*
Lesson Two: *Girls Respect Cool Trousers*
Lesson Three: *Play Hard to Get—It Drives Them Wild*
Lesson Four: *Presents They Will Like*
Lesson Five: *Girls Like Sports (Whatever They Might Say)*
Lesson Six: *How to Take Your Girlfriend on the Perfect Date*
Lesson Seven: *Never Spend Much Time Together—Keep Her Guessing*
Lesson Eight: *How to Ditch the Chick! (Sensitively)*
Lesson Nine: *My Life as School Heartthrob*

"So I'd appear in lesson nine?" I say.

"Yup. Alongside me, of course. Deal?"

I'd get Vanessa AND be part of a breakthrough venture in self-help publishing.

"Deal."

EIGHT

attracting girls is easy, is it?

Jack puts me straight on to lesson two. He says that lesson one is really meant for those who don't have the benefit of his personal guidance. Fair enough.

First things first. I need to LOOK cool to BE cool. Vanessa is as cool as a snowman's fridge, so to attract her I must be the same. Problem: you can't look all that cool in a school uniform. Solution: you make ADAPTATIONS.

Jack helps me by pointing out the subtle changes wrought by the school's hippest and trendiest (and therefore most popular) kids. A skewed tie here, nonregulation shoelaces there. The careful use of a pullover that's

43

just different enough in terms of exact color shade to stand out, but not different enough to arouse the attentions of the You-Don't-Come-to-This-School-Dressed Like-That Police.

So I make adaptations. Buttons undone here, shirt hanging out of the trousers there. A look that says, "Hey, I don't care what people think, I just AM."

Before school I stand on the side of the bath so I can see the whole of myself in the mirror over the sink. I definitely look . . . different. There's a definite EFFECT I've achieved here.

Hmm . . . Don't forget, I tell myself, that you're totally new to this approach, so you're bound to think you look a bit strange at first. Go with the flow. Get with the action.

I go to school. Big thumbs-up from Jack. Then Kate Stumpage spoils it a bit by running up to me and asking if I'm hurt and have I been in a fight.

"No," I protest, "this is how I dress. Go away."

My new look certainly gets me noticed. To add a frisson of danger to the whole ensemble I turn up the collar of my blazer. The effect is nothing short of electric. Before roll call on New Look, Day One, I can tell that half the class is talking about me already.

Then Vanessa arrives. My heart skips a beat as she does a sort of double take. If she'd been a cartoon character, her jaw would have hit the floor like an anvil. She comes over to me! Special detour!

"Kevin, have you been in a fight?"

"Noooo." Look around the room, casual-like. Cool, cool, cool. "I decided to, y'know, go with the flow. This is, hey, the Kevin Watts Experience."

One of her elegantly contoured eyebrows arches like a Vulcan's on *Star Trek*. "I should be careful. If you keep having these experiences, you'll be living in a nightmare world." Her head shifts back slightly on her graceful neck, and she shakes it slowly.

Oh . . .

I spend three lessons and a break time trying to put a positive spin on her reaction, but I can't. By lunch I've put everything back to normal. Well, all except the orange socks and the silver pinstripe I'd drawn down the sides of my trousers, which I can't ditch until I get home.

After the last lesson, Jack helps buck up my spirits. "It's just the first lap of the marathon, Kev. Just the start of the Kevin Watts advertising campaign. Learn from this minor setback and move on. Top marks for enthusiasm. Keep it cool."

I smile bravely. Two junior kids I've never seen before come past. One nudges the other and their smirking sends them into folds of body origami. "Yeah, that's him," says the smaller one.

I go home.

Mum comes at me with two tins of gloss paint and a determined look in her eye. She holds up the tins.

"White or magnolia? For the baseboards in the downstairs loo. I've dropped several hints to Dad about the state of those baseboards, so now I'm going to do them myself. Never mind. White or magnolia? I bought both."

I absolutely do not care one way or the other. "What's the difference?" I say, trying to appear uninterested without annoying her.

"Well, one's white and one's magnolia," she laughs. "Which do you think?"

"Either."

"But which one?"

"White."

"White," she says, in a tone of voice that's dripping with disappointment.

"No, magnolia," I say, trying to appear interested in order to avoid annoying her any further. "Magnolia. Got to be. White? What was I thinking? Magnolia."

Slight pause. "OK. If that's what you want."

Mum goes to fetch a paintbrush from the cupboard under the stairs. I slump on the sofa in the living room and stare at the ceiling. There's a tiny little crack meandering its way across the corner of the room, like the line of a river on a map. Hell, she'll be roller-brushing over that with Off-White Textured Ceiling Gunk next.

The chemical whiff of paint suddenly flicks at my nose and one of Mum's terrible disco CDs starts playing. The sound reverberates in the confined space of the downstairs loo. She won't turn it down now until Dad gets home.

I bet Vanessa's house doesn't smell of paint. I bet her mother never nags about the magnolia baseboards. I bet they don't have magnolia baseboards. I steel myself for another life-enhancing evening *chez* Watts.

On the way into school next morning, Jack and I commiserate with each other over the ghastliness of our families. This only makes us feel miserable, and we walk in silence for a while. Then the conversation switches to lesson three.

"Are you sure about this?" I say.

"Of course I'm sure," says Jack.

"But it seems to go against all common sense."

"New scientific methods and radical ideas always involve the breaking of a few rules," says Jack, finger held aloft for emphasis.

Hmm, yes, well, maybe, I suppose.

Jack detects my uncertainty. "Look at it this way," he says. "James Bond is trapped in a nuclear bunker, with a bomb about to go off, surrounded by thugs with guns, and menaced by a bloke with a gray suit and a cat. Ten seconds and he'll be strawberry jam. What does he do? Check if the blonde trembling with fright beside him would like a cup of tea? NO! He shoots people. He does not get fabulous girls by talking to them and fussing around them and asking them if they'd like to borrow his cardigan. He does his own thing. Actions speak louder than words, Kev, remember that. It's all to do with the weirdness of female psychology and animal magnetism and stuff."

So: lesson three. *Play Hard to Get—It Drives Them Wild.* We go through a full rundown before arriving in class.

I'm still not convinced, but I've agreed to place myself in the hands of the Master, and I intend to stay true to my word. Vanessa surely can't respect a man who gives up at the first hurdle?

By the end of the week, I'm still not convinced. On top of that, I'm not Mr. Popularity, either. I ignore pretty much anyone female, exactly as directed. Upon the approach of said female persons, I look in the other direction, start to whistle, begin talking loudly to a male colleague about boys' subjects, and employ other similar playing-hard-to-get strategies. I sit with only Jack at lunchtimes. I answer requests for loans of textbooks or test answers with nothing but a lofty indifference.

None of this appears to drive the girlies wild as promised. On the contrary, I appear to have acquired a couple of new nicknames among the girls, in which the words "snotty" and "creep" seem to figure prominently.

Vanessa keeps giving me looks that are nothing short of alarming. Looks that say "You're strange" in Day-Glo, twenty-meter-high capital lettering. Finally, she says to me (from a distance), "Is there some problem we should be making allowances for? Divorcing parents? Dental hygiene crisis?"

"I'm supposed to be expressing my moody side," I say. "I'm rejecting conventional social behavior and getting in touch with the world of instinct."

"You're certainly in touch with the world of being-a-toffee-nosed-sod," says Vanessa sweetly.

Now, correct me if I'm wrong here, but so far all my efforts seem to be having the opposite effect to the one intended. I have actively put Vanessa OFF me. And I am a toffee-nosed sod.

At home, I'm briefly distracted by the free CD-ROM taped to the cover of this month's *Mac Hardware*. I say briefly, but I'm at my keyboard until teatime. I have a go at a playable game demo and get quite good at steering my submarine away from savage aquatic dinosaurs.

Computers have the ability to distort time: each *appar-*

ent ten minutes you spend trying out free software and cleaning up your system extensions actually equals forty-five minutes of real time. For a while, I'm completely absorbed in updating my Web browser, but an earful from Mum about eyestrain from staring at screens soon snaps my mind back to the events of the day. I realize I'm still feeling silly.

I fume for a couple of hours and then I phone Jack.

"Lessons two and three are duff!" I whine.

"Do not give in to the Way of Despair, little one," Jack counsels. "You're going too far, too fast. That's all. You've got to do these things in a measured, sophisticated way. Learn, apply, maneuver. Gotta go, I'm taking Michelle from Ten A out for a pizza, and I'm looking forward to extra toppings, if you get my drift. RrrrrRRRrrrr."

I mull things over during a long bath. Maybe Jack's right. I can't simply go—zap!—changing myself like that. It's too obvious, it's too extreme. Or perhaps it's only too obvious the way I'VE been doing it. Trouble is, subtlety's never been my strong point.

In the end, I decide to try applying reverse psychology to the problem. As of the next morning, I'm outgoing, I'm interested in what other people have got to say, and I am officially God's gift to the friendly smile.

At first, I worry that I'm going too far again and that I'm straying into Gregory Timms's Geeksville. But no, people are amused (yeah, go on, have a laugh at me, you swine) but polite. Kate Stumpage goes on and on about how important it is to get in touch with your inner self and how you can't do that without trying things out and seeing what suits you first. I suppose she's only trying to be helpful.

And Vanessa talks to me again! We hold a short conversation between math and English about how it can't be long before 35mm film is as dead as a doornail, and how we won't give a damn. She smiles at me a couple of times, like she's pleased to see me! And I walk beside her, and suddenly I feel OK again.

And then . . . !

Joy!

Oh, how fickle is fate! Yesterday: ruination. Today: the world is a wonderful place. Why?

We're going in through the double doors of the main building. There's the usual crush of kids. Mr. Arbuthnott, head of geography, is breaking up a swordfight with rulers in the corridor. There are shouts and chants. Vanessa is slightly ahead of me now. She turns and calls above the noise:

"By the way, would you like to come over to my house? Saturday night, about eight?"

Sixteen words have changed my life. Every molecule of my insides explodes with light.

Just like that.

Sixteen words. Just like that.

"YES!" I cry, nodding as well, just in case the swordfight drowns out the word itself. "YES."

She smiles and nods. OK, fine, see you there. She tells me her address and then says, "Actually, I don't know if—"

Then her voice is drowned out for three or four seconds

because Mr. Arbuthnott has just gone down fighting and there's a fresh surge of shouts.

But I don't need to hear. I don't need anything anymore. For if I die at this very moment, I die a happy man.

I am going to her house, Saturday night, about eight.

I have a DATE with Vanessa Wishart.

NINE

that went really well, don't you think?

Saturday night. About eight.

I recognize her street from that photo in her project. Halfway along it, I wander out to the white dotted line in the middle of the road and crouch down.

This is where she took it from. I smile to myself. You don't get a view of this place anything like that from anywhere else but here. I'm in awe of the kind of talent it takes to spot something like that, although I have to admit her style still seems a shade too quirky for me. After all, if I was framing this street, I'd probably have more sky and maybe—

A Ford comes hurtling up behind me and honks me into

a star shape about six meters off the ground. It weaves away into the distance.

"You blithering idiot!"

Sorry.

I strut my stuff to number thirty-eight. All the houses in this street are detached, and not one of them looks like any of the others. Now, that's class.

Vanessa's house is double-fronted, with an irregular shape that gives the roof an angular, mountain-range look. Tall sash windows smile down at me from regular intervals.

It's a warm evening, and the lazy slant of the sun is throwing hazy reds and oranges around the sky. The green of leaves and the yellow of flowers and the gray-brown of birds all dot the world in different wavelengths of light and shade.

I'm wearing a carefully selected mix of casual and smart attire. I look gooood. No, really, I do.

I approach the navy blue front door. If my heart pounds any harder it'll be visible through my shirt.

Maybe she'll show me into the front room, where I'll meet her parents and make them laugh with a few well-chosen witticisms. Maybe she'll guide me through her photographic portfolio. Maybe we'll talk and talk, and smile. Maybe, as I leave, wafted on the bliss of her beauty, I'll overhear a proud father congratulate his daughter on her choice of boyfriend, and maybe add something in a twinkly voice about excellent fiancé material.

From my pocket, I produce the bar of expensive Swiss chocolate I've brought for her. Just a little pressie. Nothing over the top. Nothing that reveals I'm a lovesick puppy dog. Just something small, something inconsequential, something a tiny bit less obvious than flowers, to say "thanks" and "let's do this again sometime."

Deeeeeng deeernnnnnng.

Wow. Even her doorbell's gorgeous.

A few seconds of silence, then Vanessa flings the door open and gives me a huge grin. "Hiya! Come on in!" She's wearing a sleek green knee-length dress and her feet are bare. I fight back the urge to fall at them.

Behind her, framed in the tall rectangle of the doorway, is an interior straight out of a fashion magazine. No DIY phone table, no it'll-do-for-now carpet, no magnolia base-boards. It's all tasteful wood and wallpaper.

Then I notice Vanessa's holding what appears to be a large paper cup. From behind her rolls a wave of pop music. And voices.

I stumble inside and she closes the door behind me. The hallway is wide and bright, with a long stairway to one side and open doors on the other, through which the noise is flowing. Above the stairs, stickied to the ceiling on strands of cotton, is a swirl of streamers and balloons, along with a banner saying, in multicolored letters, "HaPpY BiRtHdAy!!!"

Oh . . .

. . .

. . . Christ . . .

"You didn't have any trouble finding us, did you?" she says, leaning toward me to speak above the music. She smells heavenly.

"Er, no," I say weakly. "No trouble."

She spots the chocolate. I hand it to her at arm's length as if I'm some bloomin' toddler. "Oh! Thanks!"

Oh, God! "It'snotyourbirthdaypresent!" I blurt out. Think,

man, THINK! "That's . . . outside! It's a surprise!" WHAT?? NO!! You PRAT!!

Her eyes flash huge for a second. "Outside? It must be something special?"

Kevin Watts, you are a BLITHERING IDIOT! Oh, God, where's lesson four when you need it?

"Aha," I gasp feebly, "you'll just have to wait and see."

We go through into the lounge. About a dozen people are lounging about. Including Kate Stumpage (!) and James (!!!!!!!) and a few others from our class, plus one or two I don't know. Everyone's body language has been translated into social dialect, full of hand gestures and pretend surprise. I presume that the ones I don't know are old friends of Vanessa's from London. The overdressed style of their clothes labels them as a bunch who secretly think they're slumming it and ought to stick together.

Kate gives me a little wave and slugs back her drink. Half a dozen of the London mob are dancing like mad over by the hi-fi.

It's Vanessa's . . . birthday party. HOW THE HELL DID I MISS THAT ONE? WHAT IN THE NAME OF—

My stomach does an inside-out flop as I remember the three or four seconds I didn't hear what she said, when she asked me, "Actually, I don't know if . . ."

. . . you realize it's my birthday . . .

Vanessa points me in the direction of a table full of drinks while she goes off to "sort out the food." The drinks are all jugs of colored liquid and three-liter plastic bottles and nonalcoholic wine. Oh, so her parents must be in, then.

Everyone's chattering and laughing. Except me. At least I'm appropriately dressed . . . as if that's any kind of consolation.

I gulp down a cup of ginger beer and try to look like someone whose dreams haven't been cruelly blasted into a billion pieces.

Suddenly, Kate's at my side. She starts hanging off my shoulder.

"Kevin, I like your shirt."

"Thanks . . . I like . . ." I take a quick look at her. Even I know you don't put four types of pink together. ". . . your shoes." God, the shoes are pink too.

"You seem very nervous, Kevin. I hope I'm not sending you all of a dither. I mean, here we all are, away from school, away from our usual environment. You know, in a more adult situation, and, well, it's the sort of situation in which our feelings might run away with us."

Why can't she EVER take a hint? She forces you either to go along with her pink-romance-fairy-cake world or shatter it by being blisteringly rude, just to get through to her. Walking the diplomatic tightrope is wearing me out.

"You're not sending me all of a dither. I'd have noticed."

"OK," she says quietly, smiling. She tries to engage me in interesting trivia about pop music, but my attention keeps wandering. She pulls her lips into a couple of weird squiggles as she sips at her nonalcoholic wine. "Urgh, this stuff's horrible."

"Then why are you drinking it?"

She tuts at me. "Because it's got the word 'wine' on the label. Gawd, you're so unsophisticated. Have you met Vanessa's parents yet?"

"No," I say, looking around the room. The dancing people in the corner are squabbling over which CD to put on next. James is telling a small audience of girls the full story of the rugby team's thirty-six-nil triumph over St. Egbert's School. A story told in the inimitable short-sentence, low-syllable-count James style. They're not listening anyway, they're gazing vacantly into his baby-blue eyes.

"Are you listening?"

"Huh?"

"I said Vanessa's mum is just like she is on telly, only shorter," says Kate. "And her dad is quite charming, really."

"Really?" I say, totally uninterested.

No, wait!

Wait!

There could yet be a glimmer of hope left in this ghastly situation! If her parents are here, I should turn that fact to my advantage. Brilliant! Even Jack would be impressed. For a start, I can make absolutely sure I make a good impression on both of them. It can't hurt to have them on my side. That way, at least I'll stand out from the crowd.

Brilliant!

I spin Kate around on her pink high heels. "Her dad's a writer, isn't he?" I say.

"Yes," says Kate, suddenly beaming at me. "Haven't you read any of his books? *The Village*? *The Stone Boat*? *Under the Green Dome*? I read them all, ages ago."

I memorized the titles, secret-agent style. "Nope. Never heard of them. What are they about? Pretend you're in English lit. Quick synopsis."

"Er, let's see. *The Stone Boat* is about smugglers in the eighteenth century. *The Village* is this mystery about a deserted village. That won a big award. And—"

"Shhh!" I hiss. Out of the corner of my eye I can see Vanessa coming back. She glides through the room like a sports car glides round corners.

"There's food in the kitchen, everyone," she announces. "Help yourselves."

The dancing people break off from their squabble and make a dash for the kitchen. Everyone else eventually heads that way, so I do too.

Vanessa's parents are there. Her mum does indeed look shorter than she looks onscreen. You can tell at a glance she's the sort of person who thinks wearing a suit and a pearl necklace is slobbing out. Up close, she looks more like Vanessa than she does onscreen too. Suddenly, all I can think about is that crappy film she was in where she murders her husband and flushes him down the drain in little pieces.

"Hey, Mum, this is Kevin, the one I was telling you about," says Vanessa.

She's talked about me! She's TALKED ABOUT ME!

"Oh, yes!" says her mum. "The photographer. Hallo."

"Hi."

Long silence. And still all I can think about is that crappy film she was in where she murders her husband and flushes him down the drain in little pieces. Oh, for God's sake, MAKE A GOOD IMPRESSION!

"I enjoy your acting," I blurt out. "Very much."

"Thank you," she says warmly.

"Except, obviously, that one where you murder your husband and flush him down the drain in little pieces."

"Obviously, yes," she says icily.

Vanessa starts putting on a silly cackle and pointing a

wiggly finger at her mum. Oh God, I've opened up some hideous family wound!

"Told you, Mum. You'll never escape it."

The look her mum gives me seems to remove all traces of moisture from the room. "Well, the money was good, Kevin," she says dryly.

Hellhellhell! Move on! Move on!

Vanessa's dad has slightly tinted specs and is wearing a chunky pullover and black jeans. He would be perfect for the role of Nazi Scientist Hiding Out in Suburbia Disguised as Nice Dad. I am terrified.

"This is my dad," says Vanessa.

"H'lo, young man. Who are you, then?"

Name, rank, serial number. "Kevin."

"Kevin what?" he barks.

"Watts," I say.

"I said 'Kevin what?'" he barks loudly. He turns to Vanessa. "This boy's hard of hearing."

Time to strike! "I've read your books," I say confidently. He pauses, then nods, clearly expecting more. Aha! And more he shall get! Kevin Watts, literary critic, goes in for the kill! "Yes, I have to confess I've only recently discovered your work, but I've been absolutely loving it."

"Really?" he growls.

"Oh, yes. I thought *Under the Green Dome* was marvelous. I'm hoping it'll be on the A-level syllabus, you know, when I get to the twelfth grade. It's a book everyone should study. And I just finished *The Stone Boat* the other day. Fantastic. I could almost smell those eighteenth-century smugglers. And my copy of *The Village* is by my bedside as we speak, ready for me to dive in the minute I get home. I love mystery stories. Reeeeally looking forward to it."

He goes quiet. So does Vanessa. For a moment, I worry that I've laid it on a bit thick, gone a bit too far praise-wise and embarrassed him. But then, phew, I realize I haven't:

"How old are you, boy?" says Vanessa's dad.

"Fifteen," I say brightly.

"And you're still reading books written for eight-year-olds?" He turns to Vanessa. "This boy's an idiot."

"Dad!" hisses Vanessa. She escorts me away. "Sorry, it's nothing personal. He's like that with everyone." But I can tell she's got a more polite version of his last question in her mind.

I try to think of something devastatingly witty to say, by way of explanation. Can't manage it. My throat has closed up and my cheeks have been fitted with their own central heating.

By the time I've regained my senses and brought my shaky left knee under control, Vanessa is off in a little huddle of people standing with plates and cups poised in a way I'd be sure to make a mess of. I decide to go and give Kate a poke in the eye instead. I pull her away from holding James spellbound with interesting trivia about the Rugby World Cup.

"When exactly did you read Vanessa's dad's books?" I say.

"Ages ago, I told you," she says. "Ooooh, seven or eight years. But it's wonderful how they stay in your mind. He must be such an intelligent and passionate man."

"Wonderful, yeah," I say drearily.

Kate scoots off for more food. I don't know where she

puts it all. For a minute or two, I'm socially adrift. I'm not friendly enough with anyone in my immediate vicinity to go over and start talking. Got to DO something quickly, or I'll look like a right nerd.

I suddenly spot a coffee table over in the corner of the room. There are presents piled up on it.

My blood runs colder than a teacher's. I've got to sort the pressie problem out!

Can I dash out and buy something now? No.

Can I run home and wrap something up and pretend I've just bought it? No time. Nothing in my house worth giving her, anyway.

I wander casually over to the coffee table, picking up another glass of ginger beer along the way. I swig it and hum in a completely nonsuspicious way to myself. Under cover of taking a nose at the hi-fi system (very nice indeed—DAB tuner, the lot!), I sneak a look at the pile of presents.

I often find that the way people wrap pressies up says a lot about them. You can almost identify the sender by the paper and whether they put one of those little sticky bows on or not. There are several very girlie-looking parcels, and one or two that are obviously CDs. Then one catches my eye: a thinnish, rectangular box, neatly wrapped, blue stripey paper, no bow. There's just a small gift tag. I turn it over.

"To Vanessa—Happy Birthday—From K"

K! Just K. It's perfect. No, it's fate. Fate has placed THIS present on THIS coffee table, where I'd find it. It's clearly from one of the other boys here. No girl would wrap a gift like this. And if it's from one of the boys, what would it be? Glossy photo paper for her inkjet printer, maybe? New camera strap? Something straightforward like that. Vanessa will open it, perhaps tomorrow morning after breakfast, and think of me. . . .

Yes, I KNOW it's wrong, I know it's cheating, but desperate times call for desperate measures. That what's they say, isn't it?

Act NOW, before it's too late! Before someone sees me!

I whip a ballpoint from my jacket pocket and add "evin" after the "K." I stand up, slowly, slowly, so as not to attract attention. I gulp down the last of my ginger beer and walk away, casually, casually.

Whether it's nerves, or whether it's the three liters of ginger beer that my nerves have made me drink, I suddenly need a wee. Up the stairs, on the right, says one of the dancing people.

It's very quiet up the stairs, on the right. The bathroom cuts out the music and the chattering from below. A little haven of peace in this whole wretched evening. I breathe deeply a few times, and feel a bit calmer.

Even their bathroom is gorgeous. Tasteful, aqua-colored tiles, surrounding one of those old-fashioned metal baths with the animal-claw feet. The lighting is bright, but not glaring. And good grief, it's true—there's a shelf above the towel rail with her mum's awards on it!

I have my wee, pull the flush and pick up an Emmy. Hmm, surprisingly heavy. I make a short acceptance speech into the mirror.

"I'd like to thank the academy . . . It's such an honor to be voted Best Performance in Love with Vanessa Wishart . . ."

I replace the award on the shelf in a silent and reverential manner. Then I quickly check my trousers. No splashes. My hair? Couple of smooth-downs, and it's fine. OKaaaay.

I saunter downstairs, whistling casually. No problemo.

I judge that it's time to leave. While I'm ahead.

The trouble is, by the time I get back down, there's a definite movement of people into the front room. I can't go now without looking obvious.

I follow in behind Kate, who would be crawling around on her hands and knees if the amount of wine she's drunk hadn't been entirely fun-free. To my horror, I discover that people are watching Vanessa open her presents.

No, wait, don't panic. The real pressie-giver might have left already . . . Or . . . He might have sent it along with a friend, because he couldn't be here himself. . . . On second thoughts, panic.

The girls are the ones who are enjoying the show. Girls don't seem to have any inhibitions about going "Ooooh" and "That's REALLY nice, I'd like one of those." Vanessa is most of the way through the presents already. Exactly as I predicted: balanced mix of CDs, photo paper, etc.

She gets to a small one with a huge yellow bow on it. It is perhaps the girliest-looking of the whole lot. She reads the card that is taped to it and looks over at the girl-swarmed rugby player standing by the drinks table.

"Aww, thanks, James," she says.

"That's from me," says James, pointing at the pressie.

Oh, shut up.

She opens it. Jeeezus, it's photo-cataloging computer software! Damned expensive software at that!

"Fantastic," breathes Vanessa. With her leaning over the box like that, I can almost . . . "I've been meaning to get something like this for ages. Thank you so much!"

Then she gets up, very deliberately, crosses the room

63

and plants a smacker on James's cheek. I feel faint for a second or two. Wolf whistles come from the back of the room.

James is giving her one of his devastating smiles, the miserable, low-down sewer rat. I notice that Vanessa's mum and dad have slipped into the crowd and are now perched behind their daughter.

Next to last pressie: mine! My leg seems to have started shaking again.

"Ooh, that's from me!" pipes up Kate at my shoulder. Now my other leg's started shaking too.

Vanessa glances at the tag and looks up. "Oh, and from Kevin. I didn't know the two of you were a couple." Louder wolf whistles come from the back, plus a handful of kissy-kissy noises.

A long arm entwines itself around mine. Kate hops up on tiptoe to whisper in my ear. "Neither did I," she says.

"Er . . ."

"Did you sneak your name onto that pressie, Kev?" she says.

Blast her innate perceptiveness of human frailty! Her eyes are all aglitter.

I give her a feeble smile. I can't do much else, can I?

She walks her fingers along my shoulder. "I ought to be very, very cross with you. But I'm not. It's because you're shy, isn't it? It's your way of telling me you fancy me."

Vanessa is pulling the wrapping paper apart.

"I sensed it all along," says Kate. "I can tell when great emotions are tormenting a soul. It's a natural gift of mine. And your soul is definitely in torment."

The wrapping paper is off. Vanessa lifts the lid off the

64

plain white box inside and pulls out a tissue-wrapped selection of designer underwear. Typical bloody Kate.

For maybe three seconds, or maybe for half a lifetime, there is silence.

"Thank you," says Vanessa.

"He chose them," sniggers Kate, pointing at me. That's what passes for her sense of humor.

"That boy's a pervert," mumbles Vanessa's dad.

TEN

i am a rugby-playing cool kid

I know it's coming. I rehearse my sarcastic answers all day Sunday, but then, when it finally does come, on Monday morning, I go all to pieces and can't do the frosty stare I've been trying out in the hall mirror.

"You gonna ask Vanessa Wishart if she's wearing your undies then, mate?"

I receive sixteen variations on that theme before the end of break time: five of them from kids I've never even seen before; two from shorty juniors who shouldn't speak to their elders and betters like that; one from Fat Lunch Lady, who then laughs like she's Mrs. Comedy.

Vanessa herself seems OK about it. I manage to blurt

out ten-second groveling apologies in the gaps between morning lessons.

Well, she SAYS she's OK about it, but there's a sort of undertone in her voice. I've upset her in some way, I can tell, but what I can't tell is whether it's because of the undies or not.

Things aren't made any easier by having Kate Stumpage hanging around me all the time. She keeps making comments about the depth of my feelings and the twin bluey-gray pools of my eyes. This girl doesn't want a boyfriend, she wants a giant tin of golden syrup. I don't mean to be unkind, but REALLY . . . !

I manage to give her the slip at lunchtime and engage Vanessa in proper conversation during apple pie and custard.

"K-Kate bought them," I stammer. "Honest, I had no idea—"

Vanessa holds up a hand. A pale, slender hand I long to hold in mine. "Forget it," she says. "I've told you, it's irrelevant. I. Am. Not. Offended. OK? Just drop it."

"I mean, it's not that I couldn't be bothered to go out and choose you a pressie. It's not that. It's that, well, obviously Kate and I discussed at great length . . . No! We didn't discuss anything! She just went ahead and—"

Vanessa gives me a goggle-eyed look and runs thumb and forefinger across her mouth like a zip.

"I'll shut up," I say.

Kate has tracked me down. She plonks her tuna-salad thing on the table and squeezes up next to me. I try to edge her off the bench, but she's having none of it. She flips her head to one side to see round me.

"Have you got any idea who did it yet?" she says in a conspiratorial giggle.

"No," says Vanessa, smiling. She's suddenly trying to suppress a huge laugh.

"Done what?" I say, intrigued, looking back and forth between them. Hey, pleeeeease let it be that James got caught nicking something!

"After the party, we realized that someone must have done the old acceptance-speech-into-the-mirror bit with one of Mum's awards," says Vanessa, having a difficult time keeping that laugh down.

"How on earth could you possibly know?" I say.

"They replaced it back to front," says Vanessa. "We had a theater director over to dinner once who did the same thing. He still doesn't know we know."

"What a saddo," smirks Kate.

"I laughed till my sides hurt," says Vanessa, "but Mum was furious."

"She should have called the police," pipes up Kate. "Whoever did it might be a bit strange. You know, an obsessive fan or something. It shows a complete lack of respect for other people's property."

"Why don't you push off?" I grumble.

"Is that the way you talk to all your girlfriends?" says Vanessa, archly.

"No! Just her! I mean, she's not my girlfriend!"

"Then why are you buying birthday presents together?"

"He works in mysterious ways," mouths Kate, wrinkling up her nose and giving me a hug. "Shy people are often like that."

I take refuge with Jack. After hearing a full account of

Saturday night, and after a further twenty minutes spent laughing until he chokes, Jack provides counsel.

"Do something personal," he says.

"Personal . . . ," I say, requiring rather more counsel than that.

"We are are deep into the territory of lesson four, my pupil," says Jack.

"Frankly, Jack, I'm rapidly losing faith in your methods."

He pulls up his legs and sits in what I assume is meant to be an Eastern-style lotus position but which would be better named as "trampled undergrowth."

"Do not waver from the true path, Kev-boy. Don't give up now. Beware, for lesson four is the single trickiest area in the entire science of girlfriend management. Buying things. Think a box of chocolates is a safe bet? Think again! She might say, 'Oh, thank you, my darling, this is the loveliest pressie I've ever had.' As of course she should. BUT she might equally say, 'Thanks a heap, you rotten dirtbag, bang goes my diet, are you trying to make me fat?' You never know which you're going to get. Although in either case she'll definitely offer you the ones she doesn't like, so get used to coffee creams."

"But what's personal about a box of chocolates?"

Jack raises his hand in a particularly spiritual way. "It's all relative, Kev. The principle applies to almost any form of gift. The only way to increase your chances of a good response is to make your offering as personal as possible. Something unique to you. Something she can treasure. I gave Lisa in Nine M my old denim jacket, for instance."

"The one with all the stained bits at the back?" I gasp.

"Yup."

"But you loved that jacket."

"I did, Kev, I did. However, it was getting too small for me. Too small for me, BUT the right size for a girl. She was stunned when I gave it to her. Speechless. A personal gift, you see. It cuts short all criticism. You can't go far wrong."

You've got to admit, it's a very interesting concept. And with Vanessa and me sharing a hobby, coming up with a fantastic idea takes me no more than three and a half nanoseconds. Perhaps the Jack program deserves another chance.

The following morning, I'm extremely tired and extremely pleased with myself. Tired because I've been slaving over a hot computer till three in the morning. Pleased because rolled up inside my schoolbag is the result of all my endeavors.

I'd taken one of the (ahem, many) shots I'd got of Vanessa and photoedited it to within an inch of its life. It was now a soft-focus masterpiece of pastel shades, hearts and flowers. A bit girlie, yeah, OK, I admit, but girls like hearts and flowers, AND it's an absolutely personal and true reflection of my feelings. Feelings that, once Vanessa has been bowled over by my gift, I can maybe, perhaps, possibly begin to express.

I'm slightly late into class. Everyone's already there. I need to find a quiet minute when I can speak to Vanessa alone and present her with my tribute. I must bide my time, not rush things, choose exactly the right moment. . . .

Vanessa and some of the other girls are giggling over something in a magazine. Most of them are making ukk-ukk throwing-up noises too.

"Just how far under the age of ten do they think we are?" says Vanessa. "Eurgh, hearts and flowers, yuck!"

"Are we all going to watch the rugby team trials tomorrow?" says Kate.

"Yyyyyep," chorus the others.

I turn right around, leave the room, rip my tribute into several thousand pieces and squash it down in the overflowing bin outside the science block.

Lesson four: dead duck. However, this time it isn't really anyone's fault. I simply approached the idea from the wrong angle, that's all. Unfortunately, that angle was the only one I had.

I contemplate lesson five for a while. It seems too drastic. After all, when it comes to sports I'm normally the one who gets picked for a team only one kid ahead of Gregory Timms. I'm not exactly known for my athletic prowess.

But, then, on the other hand, I could do with getting more exercise. Mum's always telling me to go out and get some fresh air. And, you never know, it might just broaden my horizons, or give me a whole new hobby, or something like that.

OK, fine. Time for something more drastic. Lesson five. But let me make this absolutely clear: this is the Jack method's last, final, draw-the-line, no-extensions chance.

So. If Vanessa's going to give kisses on the cheek to the likes of James the rugby player, then perhaps I should become Kevin the rugby player!

I volunteer for the rugby team trials. The sports staff at this school take their jobs far too seriously, and are forming their under-sixteens El-Brutalismo Kamikaze Squad for the autumn term even though it's only May. What a fun summer they're going to have.

Anyway, I add my name to the list on the main notice board (should have realized what I was up against when I noticed that James's was the most legible handwriting after mine). The next day, I squeeze into last year's sports gear and turn up at lunchtime.

There's a small crowd of girls on the touchline. Well, a small crowd of girls and Gregory Timms. I'm getting worried about him. Vanessa is among the girls. Under any other circumstances I'd have felt put off—I mean, if a small crowd of boys turns up to watch the girls' netball practice they get chased off by Miss Gretchen, queen of the boilersuit.

The whistle blows. All the other guys are twice my size but I'm determined to stand my ground. I've got speed on my side, and maneuverability, and superior tactical thinking.

I regain consciousness in the sick room. At first, I assume that the shaven-headed figure floating in front of me is some sort of St. Peter of the rugby world, but it's only Miss Gretchen.

"How many fingers am I holding up, Watts?" she barks.

I have no idea. "Less than ten?"

"That'll do. Get back to your class."

OK, rugby's out. James gets made captain for the next school year, by the way. Again.

Why the hell did I ever think I could compete on a physical level? My mind must be more addled than I thought.

I absolutely KNOW my mind is addled when I get my latest history essay back. History is a subject I like: you know where you are with it. It's not like physics or math—there aren't any viciously complicated versions of history that you know are waiting to squeeze your brain in a few terms' time. You don't get people studying advanced history or differential history, do you? With history, it's all just down to how much detail you get into.

So when this essay comes back with a D-minus slapped in marker pen at the top, I'm genuinely irritated. In the margins: "Don't understand your point," "This is muddled," "Much more needed here," blah blah blah. I'm GOOD at history. I did the reading. I know as much about the Industrial Revolution as anyone in this class, go on, test me, ask me a question!

After a couple of days of inward sulking, I'm forced to admit to myself that the new me is still nowhere in sight. Vanessa is a highly intelligent person and I'm certainly not going to win her heart while she sees me trailing at the bottom of the class, am I? I must put renewed effort into my studies!

Aha! Maybe I could sweep to a towering academic victory and thus impress Vanessa with the raw power of my brain? Not the way my schoolwork's going at the moment, I couldn't. But I COULD do it, I know I could! I have to concentrate.

So, one thing's for sure. Lessons six, seven, eight and nine can go take a running jump. "I'm sorry, Jack, I'm leaving the program."

Jack squishes his lips and lets out a long, slow breath. "Can't say I'm not disappointed, Kev. I mean, you've not exactly fulfilled your vow yet, have you? You've not exactly hit the jackpot."

"No, thanks to lessons two, three, four and five."

"You've got to remember you're still a humble apprentice. It takes practice and dedication to attain my level of competence. Believe it or not, even I wasn't perfect straight out of the starting gate. It could take a dozen girls or more to get things running smoothly."

"I don't want a dozen girls or more," I moan. "I want THIS girl."

He shrugs. "You'll be back."

"No, I won't."

He shrugs again. "Your loss."

I pass the main notice board again the next day. In the sectioned-off bit that's labeled "Community" in blue paper cut-out letters there's a flyer about a photo exhibition in the tiny art gallery that's next to the public library.

Photo exhibition . . .

. . . Photo . . . Exhibition . . .

Innocent dating opportunity!

You see? Stuff lesson six! I can do it myself!

I don't even think about it. A more sensible and determined version of me suddenly emerges from inside my rugby-battered exterior.

I sit one desk away from Vanessa in French. While Miss DuBois is distracted by a diagram and is cheerfully shredding the language through the clogged filter of her accent, I lean over to Vanessa: "Did you see the thing on the notice board? About a photo exhibition?"

"Yes. I thought I'd go."

"Do you want to go with me?"

"OK. Friday?"

"OK."

There you go. Easy peasy.

ELEVEN

frothy cappuccino latte,
low-fat mocha espresso, please

She looks divine. She always looks divine, but tonight she looks even more diviner than ever. We're on a date. It IS a date. We're going somewhere, together, as friends of the opposite gender. That's a date.

She's tied her hair back into a bouncy little ponytail thing. It shows off the sculptured lines of her face. She's wearing a flowing something that looks very fashionable, although I have no idea what it's called, and sandals with straps that curl around her ankles.

We meet outside the gallery. The low-slung sun, huge and flat and orange, peeks through the branches of the trees that line the street. The air is dense and still, gently exhaling the heat of the day. A knot of little black insects tussles in the shade of the leaves.

We go inside. A large hand-painted notice sits on an easel in the foyer, proclaiming: "Selections from the Work of Twelve Local Professional Photographers. Prints of All Exhibits Are Available for Purchase. Please Take a Leaflet."

I want to take her hand, but a sudden pounding of my heart tells me not to, and I stuff my fists in my pockets instead. We enter a long, low room, with windows down one side and framed pictures dotted all over the other.

For several meters, nothing much grabs our attention. We're the only people here, apart from a dubious-looking old bloke in the far corner, who's paying minute attention to an enormous photo of a dubious-looking old lady. Our footsteps ka-klack loudly on the varnished wooden floor.

Vanessa stops and points. "There, look at that."

It's a color picture of the town hall, taken in low light. The blues in the sky are exaggerated, and the perspective is slightly forced. Taken with maybe a 20mm lens to get a wider angle of view. You can tell from the way the enhancements look that there were filters over the lens. It wasn't done electronically, the way I'd have done it. My guess is that it was taken on old-fashioned film. A bit dull, but well done, I think.

"Hmm," I say.

"Isn't it awful?" says Vanessa.

"Absolutely." Notice there how I told a total lie to get on her good side?

"It's a local government building, for heaven's sake. Whoever took this has made it look like some chocolate-box wedding photo."

"Maybe they're just in love with the concept of local government buildings?"

She smiles at me. It sets my very soul aglow.

"I wish I could be as forgiving as you. This sort of thing really irritates me. It's not a picture of the subject. It's a picture of the photographer. It's all about THEM, and not about IT."

"But we've all got a personal style. You've definitely got a personal style. I've got a personal style."

"Yes," she says, "but you've got to choose subjects that SUIT your style. The WAY you take the picture's got to complement what's IN it. This person's style is similar to yours. Bright colors and so forth. Perfect for baby pictures and summer meadows. And look what it's a picture of!"

I feel like I've been told off. An unkind thought about Vanessa's photographic style being perfect for a war correspondent flashes through my mind. I brutally suppress it at once.

But she's got a fair point. I have taken photos of babies.

"Haven't you ever taken a photo of a baby?" I ask.

"Once. For the people we used to live next door to. It was rubbish. I made the kid look like he was about to cry. Still, it taught me to know my limits. You've got to be true to yourself, haven't you?"

I can see what she means. Suddenly, she twirls on her heels and covers her eyes.

"I haven't read the caption, honest! See if I'm right! I BET you this was taken by someone who's been on the local paper since the dawn of time."

I have to stand closer and bend at the knee to read the tiny print on the rectangle of card beneath the picture. She is absolutely right. Mr. Tony Barstow has been in the employ of the *Evening Herald,* in the position of staff photographer, since the year of our Lord nineteen hundred and sixty-three.

"Told you," she says, shaking her head. "You can tell a mile off."

We hardly stop talking all the way through the gallery. We hardly stop talking all the way back out of the gallery and off along the street toward the shopping center. She grabs my arm and lets out a mock Holy Cow! gasp.

"Did you hear? Pewsey had me in his office yesterday afternoon."

"Oh, hell! Why?"

She grins. "Some charity or other is sponsoring 'Inspirational, Atmospheric Public Art in Schools.'" She flicks inverted commas in the air and pulls a yuck-face. "So, of course, Pewsey wants a huge photo of himself in the lobby of the main hall."

"Ooooh my gaaaaaad."

"Precisely. But it's a real commission, I actually feel flattered. I'm going to get a brass plaque next to the picture, with my name on it."

"Even Doisneau and Cartier-Bresson had to start somewhere."

"Right. I'm supposed to go and snap him posing by his desk after half term, but he's leaving the choice of picture up to me. He says he saw my stuff in that art project we all did the other week." Then she drops into a smack-on impression of the man that has me howling with laughter. "The subject matter was somewhat strange, young lady, but since in this case the subject matter will be me, I don't think we need worry. Technical competence is the important point here, and yours is clearly adequate."

For a split second, I think to myself that I ought to feel a pang of jealousy over commissions and plaques and stuff. But I don't, at all.

I have to admit, my thoughts are more on the fact that she actually touched my arm. I keep it at exactly the same angle, just in case she feels the need to grab it again for any reason.

We carry on talking. She doesn't grab my arm, but it turns out she's been to Paris, which is somewhere I've always fancied going.

"Did you have your portrait painted on the West Bank?" I say.

She raises her eyebrows. "Hardly. I'd have been too busy ducking bullets."

"Eh?"

"The West Bank is in the Middle East," she says in a stage whisper, cupping her hand to her mouth.

DAMMIT! "I knew that," I say with a sheepish grin. "Oh, right, Paris is the LEFT Bank."

"Uh-huh."

"And the South Bank is in London . . ."

"Uh-huh."

"So where did the North Bank go?"

"There's the National Westminster Bank." She shrugs. "Or a blood bank."

"Or a bottle bank."

"Or a riverbank."

"Or an armored tank."

"Or a man called Frank."

I feel a warmth that has nothing to do with the weather. Here I am, in conversation with perfection, and it's not difficult, and it's not nerve-wracking. It feels completely right.

"Shall we go for a cup of coffee?" I say.

"Sure," she says.

We bump into James on the way. DAMMIT! DAMMIT!

"Hi, James," she says, far too brightly for my liking.

"Hiya, Nessie," says James. Nessie?! Nessie, for God's sake? He chucks me a sideways glance. "H'lo, Watts. Sorry about the elbow in the neck at the rugby trials."

"Evenin'," I reply quietly.

"We're going to go and get a coffee," says Vanessa. "Do you want to come too?"

NOOOOOO!

"Cool," says James. He gives a quick tug at the collar of his bulging sports shirt and off we go.

We bump into Kate on the way. Holy Jesus, what is this? *The Wizard of Oz*? She doesn't even wait to be asked. She just tags along. If I'D done that, it would seem downright rude, but, oh no, not if it's Little Miss Happy-Go-Lucky, grumble, moan, whine . . .

By the time we get into Starbucks, I'm cheesed off enough to keep a cracker factory happy for a month. The place is packed, which doesn't help. I've never liked crowds.

There's a big board above the counter bristling with this-a-chinos and that-a-mochas. Why can't they just do instant like the rest of us?

I can't hear what the others are ordering because of the KSHHHH-ing of the coffee machines and the yattering of the customers. I don't know what an espresso is, but I've heard of it, and it sounds sophisticated, so I order one. I had no idea coffee cups could come that small.

Ah! I'm nearest the till! I do the standard no-I'll-pay routine and they do the standard are-you-sure-well-thanks routine. They take their big cups of frothy stuff (aww, cappuccino, that's what I meant) and weave their way over to the last free table.

The South American girl on the till is leaning over the counter at me, and at first I assume the figure she's shouting must be in pesos or something. But no, apparently not.

"HOW much?" I gasp.

Once my wallet's been emptied, I join the others. Dammit again, James is sitting next to Vanessa. I'm forced to sit next to Kate and she immediately entwines her arm around mine. Now I can't even drink my coffee.

"Have you two been out anywhere nice recently?" says Vanessa.

"No," I say quickly.

Kate nips at my cheek with her free hand and gives it a quick cheeky-chops wiggle. "He's so shy and sensitive, he can't even pluck up the courage to phone me, can you, Kevvie?" She suddenly throws me her little pointy-chipmunk grin and tells me I've gone her favorite shade of pink.

"Give it a rest," I mumble.

"So no phone calls, no going out," says Vanessa. "You're on to a winner there, Kate."

"Exactly what I think," I chip in. "I'm hopeless as a boyfriend, she ought to dump me right now." Oh no, no, NO! AAARgh, RATS!

"At least you're honest about it," says Vanessa with a shrug, sipping her coffee.

"I'm prepared to wait until he emerges from his shell," sighs Kate. "Like a butterfly from its chrysalis. Every horoscope I've read this month tells me love is waiting around the corner, just when I least expect it."

Then Vanessa and Kate notice what the woman at the next table is wearing, and switch into girlie talk. I free my arm and take a sip of my espresso. It is vile.

James leans over to me. He picks up a paper napkin holder from the center of the table and holds it by his face like a shield. The phrase "Don't be so blindingly obvious, you gormless great oaf" springs to mind.

"Watts," he hisses. "You take Stumpage and go. I'll tackle Wishart on me own. Think I'm on to something here. Think she fancies me."

Oh God, no.

No she doesn't.

No she doesn't.

I have a physical spasm of shock that sends a long splash of espresso plunging down my leg. Ow, that's hot! The girls haven't seen, they're still busy on lipstick or something. James is trying to work out which way round to put the napkin holder back. There's a steaming, dark stain all the way down my light brown trousers. WHY? Why me, AL-WAYS?

"James, I've got to go and get this off!" I whisper urgently. "Don't move!"

I get up and shuffle hurriedly toward the toilets. As I go James gives me a pat on the back. "Good man."

The coffee's really starting to hurt. I collapse through the swing door to the loos. Nobody about, thank goodness. I hop into a cubicle, lock the door and quickly pull my trousers off.

No actual burn on my leg, it's just a bit red. I suppose I should be grateful for small mercies. The trouser leg is soaked. How the hell did one tiny cup contain this much liquid?

I start unraveling loo roll and dabbing frantically at the stain. It's not going to come out, is it? The best I can do is dry it as much as possible and hope Vanessa doesn't notice.

Suddenly, I hear the swing door bounce back on its hinges and half a dozen female voices come in. Oi! What are they doing in the . . . ?

Great.

I'm not in the men's at all. Am I?

And I've got no trousers on.

It's OK, just stay put, and stay quiet. Wait until they go.

I silently close the lid of the loo and crouch on top of it. Now they can't see my shoes. There's nothing to give me away. I just have to stay put, and stay quiet, and wait until they go.

While I'm waiting, I read the litany of personal sorrow on the cubicle walls: "Luv U Andy Newman," "Bugz 4 Tezza," "Sara is a COW." There's an arrow drawn toward the loo roll, above which is "A-Level certificates. Please take one." A selection of shoes clop in and out of sight underneath the cubicle door. Two or three pairs of plain pumps, a pair of white scuffed sneakers, black high heels that must be agony from the way they're tottering along. Why do girls DO that? I deduce that the red sandals are attached to the loudest mouth.

After about ten minutes, I'm starting to get more than a little impatient. They don't HAVE to stand there moaning about their boyfriends. They COULD go somewhere else. My legs are going numb.

Ten minutes . . . twelve . . . fourteen. For GOD'S SAKE! I can't even get out my phone. The slightest sound echoes off the walls.

Fifteen minutes they spend moaning! Fifteen! And they don't even go for a wee! At last the swing door bumps shut. I put my trousers on, whip open the catch, dash for the door, and find our table occupied by four old ladies.

"Where did they go?" I cry, frantic. They stare accusingly at me, as if I'd just confessed to liquidizing their handbags in a blender. "The people who were here! Did you see where they went?"

"Are you with the management?" says one of the old ladies.

"We've got a complaint," says the second.

"The prices in here are shocking," says the third.

The fourth one nods vigorously in support of the other three.

I get filled in on the missing bit of the story by Kate, first thing Monday morning. They start wondering where I am, and James says I've gone home. No way, says Vanessa, he wouldn't be that rude. They send James to the men's to see if I'm there, and, of course, I'm not. He's definitely gone home, says James. Good grief, says Vanessa, he IS that

84

rude. And off they go, with James's arm around Vanessa's shoulders.

"But I forgive you, Kevvie," says Kate. "I know you can't help being timid."

"Stop calling me Kevvie."

TWELVE

the adventures of thomas the train

Of course, my every effort to explain things to Vanessa just ends up sounding like a feeble excuse. She's polite, but distant. She ends up noticeably avoiding me. And noticeably not avoiding James.

Next week is half term. Which is fine. It'll be a good cooling-off period.

I have to admit, I'm feeling slightly adrift now, with terrible pangs of thinking I should just give up once and for all. But I've left the program, and I'm not going back. That's that. Even so, lesson seven keeps worming itself into my thoughts. *Never Spend Much Time Together—Keep Her Guessing.*

On the principle that previous lessons have had an opposite effect to the one intended, I can't help wondering if Always Spend Time Together would be the best way to proceed. But I just don't know. I just don't know what to do. I certainly can't sit around waiting for a miracle.

Then, a miracle happens. On the Thursday before half term, Kate tells me that Vanessa is going away with her parents for the whole week, to a rented flat in Swanage. Apparently, her mum is preparing for some big new stage thing, and you know what actors are like, wanting their time out.

I don't realize it's a miracle until that evening, when Mum puts down her copy of *Quality Time: Important Issues in the Teenage Years* and says: "Kevin, would you like to go away during half term? Just the three of us? I thought we could go to either Swanage or the Lake District. They're Dad's favorites, and he's got the week off work."

I almost leap from my chair. Dad stirs fitfully in his sleep and shuffles around on the sofa, his slippered feet lolling over one of the arms.

"Yes!" I cry. "Let's go to Swanage!"

"Oh," says Mum. Her head does that quick little nod that means I've deviated from her carefully prepared script. "Not the Lake District?"

"No, Swanage, definitely! I want to go to Swanage! I'm one-hundred-percent set on Swanage! That's the place for me! My favorite too!"

Mum considers for a few minutes. Thoughts I will never understand do battle all over her facial muscles. "The Lake District is lovely."

"I'm sure it is," I say, "but Swanage is lovelier. Trust me."

"Are there any places we can visit in Swanage that would help with your schoolwork?" says Mum.

"What? I don't know."

"Because there are lots of houses in the Lake District connected with poets and the Brontës and people like that."

"I don't give a stuff about *Wuthering Heights,* Mum. Swanage. That's all I'm interested in."

Mum falls silent for a few minutes. "Or Cornwall? You liked Bude the other year."

"No! Muuum!" To demonstrate my absolute commitment to the concept of Swanage, I run upstairs and pack.

It's a genuine miracle. A sign from on high.

For half a second, I consider letting slip at school tomorrow that we're going to Swanage too, but then I decide against it. It would be better if Vanessa and I simply ran into each other. Hey! What a coincidence! Small world! On the beach, maybe, with her in a bikini.

Shut up! Focus!

It'd be perfect. Away from school, away from all distractions, away from (apply weedy drippy voice here) *Jaaaaaames.* Away from school, I can overcome our recent frostiness. We could take long walks along the sand, buy ice creams together, talk as the sun sets lazily in the west, throwing glittering colors across the calm waters of the bay. Spend Time Together.

And then, at the end of the week, when we were the best of friends . . .

I could tell her how I feel . . .

It would be entirely romantic . . .

I would kiss those soft and tender lips . . . And my solemn vow would be fulfilled . . .

Perfect!

All day Friday, everyone is in the grip of half term–itis, and nobody does any work. Even the teachers are watching the clock. Mr. Pewsey slopes wearily around the whole school during afternoon break, to make sure none of the staff has bunked off early.

When I get home, Mum is flicking through the pile of brochures on Dorset she's gone and got from the travel agents'. No, sorry, Mum, I am not interested in dinosaur exhibitions in Dorchester, Victorian forts in Weymouth or the natural beauty of Lulworth Cove.

"Well, what are we going to do all week?" she pipes, loud enough to cut off Dad's snoring.

"I'm a teenager, Mum. I'm gonna hang out."

"Hang out of what?" she says. "Oh, look, there's a steam railway at Swanage! Here's a picture. You used to love steam trains when you were little. We could go for a ride on that."

Over my dead body.

There's tension right up until we leave, after an early breakfast on Saturday morning. Dad whistles for the entire three hours it takes him to drive us there.

THIRTEEN

*what i did in the holidays,
by kevin watts*

Day One. Arrive at our B&B, which is quite near the waterfront. The old lady who runs it is called Mrs. Boniface, which is ironic as she is the ugliest person I have ever seen. She calls me a nice young man and asks us if we'd like to watch daytime TV with her. We hurry to the beach. I say I'm going for a walk. Mum protests that I've never voluntarily gone for a walk in my life. I protest that it's about time I did, then. Walk for miles, see no sign of a Wishart of any kind. We have fish and chips on the pier. I have a room to myself, which is good. The bed is like a slab of concrete, which is bad. Get no sleep whatsoever.

Day Two. We have breakfast in a large, sunny room in which half a dozen families attempt to eat fried tomatoes without creaking their chairs. Mrs. Boniface asks us if we'd like to listen to the news on Radio 4 with her. We hurry to the hills. Coastal paths go for miles over the cliffs. We see an interesting giant stone globe but no sign of Vanessa. Mum points out the railway station. We have chicken and chips on the pier. Get no sleep whatsoever.

Day Three. Am forced by Mum into an outing to Poole. Console myself with idea that Vanessa may also have been forced into an outing to Poole. After nine hours, can conclusively state that she hasn't been. On return to Swanage, Mum points out the railway station again. The departing steam trains give off a smell like neglected kettles. We have pie and chips on the pier. Cannot sleep for worrying.

Day Four. Manage to shake off parents at beach. Fortunately, have brought photo of Vanessa with me and can deploy it during my wanderings around the streets and boatyards of the town. Nobody recognizes her, although they are interested to hear that her mother is around here somewhere, and do I think she'd do them an autograph? We have sausage and chips on the pier. Spend night gazing wistfully at photo.

Day Five. Sudden rush of new guests means I get shifted onto the kiddies' table at breakfast. I ask runny-nosed toddler next to me if he's eating that mushroom. He says no. I eat it. Runny-nosed toddler screams. Huge scene. Mrs. Boniface asks us if we'd like to see the special features on her *Sound of Music* DVD. We hurry for the railway station. Mum delighted that resident steam train is called Thomas. Delight extends to buying tickets for entire length of branch line and back. Spend hours wedged next to excited five-year-old who clearly thinks all steam trains can talk and save their friends from dangerous situations. Am detecting a child-centered theme to this day developing. We have pineapple fritter and chips on the pier. Curse myself on another Vanessa-less day.

Day Six. Dump parents at local park, listening to brass band. Go through town with the proverbial fine-toothed comb. Gaze listlessly up at windows of every flat that looks like it might be rented. Have brilliant idea: if Wisharts are in rented flat, must be buying food from somewhere. Quiz staff in both of town's supermarkets. Blank faces all round, even when I produce photo. Staff are either on drugs or extremely stupid. Wander helplessly for a while. We have kebab and chips on the pier. Feel like crying myself to sleep, but am too damn tired.

Day Seven. Pack up car, leaving at teatime. Mum complains loudly about how we haven't done enough together as a family. I throw in towel and say how much I'd love to take in the natural beauty of Lulworth Cove. Mum says it's too late now. Argument. I storm off. I buy a computer magazine and read it on the beach. Bit windy. Presume it's all the mushrooms. Weather dreary, not many people about. Suddenly realize that huddled figure in black cardigan and dark glasses about five meters away is Vanessa. I hurry over.

"Vanessa, hi!"

She whips around in alarm, then her shoulders slump as she relaxes and she smiles at me. "Kevin! What are you doing here?"

"Aww, had a row with the old folks. Bloody parents, eh? I've just come down here to chill out."

"What, all the way to Swanage? Wouldn't your bedroom have done?"

"No, I mean, they're off buying sticks of rock candy for the people at work. We've, er, rented a flat for the week."

"Really? So have we."

"Yeah? Where exactly?" I say.

"In that block that looks out into the bay, along from the chip shop."

"Good God," I sigh. "I've been past that a hundred times."

"It's a wonder we haven't seen each other," says Vanessa. "I could have done with a friend."

Zing! Pow! Ka-splat!

Nonchalantly: "Yeah?"

"We've had a horrible time. The other day people started stopping Mum and asking for her autograph. Much more than usual, I mean. Which should have set alarm bells ringing. Then we found out that someone's been going all over the town asking about us. About Mum, and Dad, and me. Mum went berserk. She wanted to call the police but Dad said it's probably just a crank. We're having to go home this morning. Mum and Dad are in the pharmacy over there, getting something for Mum's nerves, and then we're off. I tell you, I'm starting to get really scared."

"Nooo, no, don't be scared, it's just me!"

Oh dear.

Off come the dark glasses. "What?" she says quietly. "What did you say? It's . . . YOU?" Her voice rises gradually. "Have you been FOLLOWING me? What the HELL do you think you're playing at?"

She's on her feet and advancing toward me. I'm retreating.

"What's the matter with you?" She's at the top of her voice now. "Why, for God's sake?"

Because . . .

"You must be the weirdest person I've ever met! Why do you do these weird things? WHY?"

Because . . .

Out of nowhere, her mum and dad appear. Her mum is wearing a wig, and a coat with the collar turned up. They have clearly noticed that Vanessa is not exactly pleased. They are running.

"Get away from my baby!" screams her mum.

Her dad's sleeves are rolled up and his fists are raised. "Out of the way, Vanessa, and I'll deck the bastard!" he booms.

"No! Dad! He's not worth it!" shouts Vanessa.

Her dad draws up right in front of me, snorting like a bull. His fists drop to his sides. "Oh my God, it's that idiot boy!" he barks.

Everyone along the seafront is looking at me. That runny-nosed toddler from the B&B is standing in front of the ice-cream van, licking a strawberry cone and pointing at me, glaring. You stole my mushroom.

And on Monday . . .

When I go back into school . . .

With my groveling apologies prepared . . .

I see that it's no use . . .

On the way to class I see Vanessa and James . . .

In the deep shadow between the science block and the canteen . . .

Where the kids go to smoke at break times . . .

They're kissing . . .

Kissing.

And my heart breaks in two.

FOURTEEN

one day, son, all this will be yours

My mum can never wait for Parents' Evening like a normal mother. You can see the tension building up in her over the weeks. Ooooh, how is my baby doing at school? Is his handwriting neat? Is he popular with the other boys? It usually gets too much for her shortly after half term, and this term is no exception. She cracks about a fortnight before the Parents' Evening itself.

She never actually comes out and SAYS she's been in to talk to my teachers while I'm not looking (because chapter eleven in her well-thumbed copy of *Raising a Go-Ahead*

Child says this would undermine my confidence). But you can always tell. The tension's gone, replaced by a sort of grudging acceptance. Still smack-on average in all subjects . . . Oh . . . Right . . . Fine . . . Thank you. You can read it all in her face.

This term, however, is slightly different. No grudging acceptance. Instead, there's an iron determination in her expression I've not seen since I needed to improve my math in year five. She's received the message loud and clear: Could Do Much Better. She's now in a flap about my entire future.

It makes my spirits sink even further into a pit of despair. For a couple of days I hang on, pretending I've not noticed anything, waiting for her to announce her Plan.

I know what's brought this on. My lovesickness is continuing to turn my schoolwork into a riot of red ink. I can't see the point of making the effort anymore. Wrong of me, yes, but that's how I feel.

Friday teatime. Mum attempts to sound off-the-cuff.

"Are you doing anything tomorrow, Kevin?"

" . . . Nooo."

"Oh. Would you like to go out on a couple of jobs with your dad?"

I scrape a dollop of mashed potato around my plate for a moment or two. Can't quite think round this one. "No."

"But you're not doing anything else."

"No."

"So . . . You can go with him, then."

"No."

"Why not?" she says, clearly wanting a carefully thought

out and one hundred percent watertight answer. She doesn't get one.

"I don't want to."

"You need to start thinking about career options, Kevin. There'll be serious decisions to be made before you know it. You can't rely on whatever work experience thing the school sends you on. You need proper life skills."

"But Dad's a gas fitter," I say.

"So?"

"I don't want to be a gas fitter."

"You don't know, do you, until you've tried it? You can be your dad's apprentice for the day."

"I can tell you now, Mum, gas fitting is not in my blood."

Dad comes in from the kitchen, humming tunelessly to himself. He stops dead when he sees the somewhat contrasting looks on our faces.

Next morning, Dad and I are wearing overalls and in his van by eight a.m. The first address on the corner-crumpled, handwritten job sheet is illegible, but Dad seems to know where he's going so I shut up and gaze out of the window.

The passenger seat is worn and saggy. Dad usually straps new boilers into it, in case they get damaged by bouncing around in the back with his various tool bags. The plastic and springs beneath me squeak and groan with every dip in the road, like a bag of worn-out mice gasping their last.

I watch the town zip past me. People and houses and shops and everything. It strikes me as strange that looking out at something like that should perk me up, but it always does. I think it's the way you suddenly realize that everyone else is just looking out at the people and houses and shops and everything too. Some of them are having a really horrible time, some of them are having the best time of their entire lives. But they're all having a time of some sort, and so am I. Now and again, it's nice to feel like a face in the crowd.

The van swirls around the roundabout outside Tesco, and we're heading back along a leafy, tree-lined street. One that seems very familiar.

It's Vanessa's street. I swivel into a bolt-upright position. Dear God in heaven, no. No, no, no, please don't let it be the Wishart family central heating system we've come to service. Oh dear God, no. It can't be true!

It isn't. We drive past Vanessa's house and pull into the black tarmac drive two doors down. I start breathing again.

When I think of what might have happened, the miserable, beady-eyed woman who answers the door comes as a welcome relief. She's laid a path of newspaper from her front door. Dad and I, carrying tool bags, scrunch over reports of world events to the gas fire in her living room. Somewhere at the back of the house, a very large dog is barking the canine equivalent of "Lemme at 'em."

The woman, whose name is Mrs. Something-Van-Something-Foreign, hovers around while Dad takes twenty minutes uncoupling the fire from the chimney stack and removing it to expose the back boiler. He slowly places the screws he removes in a line along the mantelpiece. Mrs. Something eyes us warily, as if she's expecting him to suddenly pocket one of her china ornaments. Eventually, she manages to tear a few words from her throat.

"Would, umm, would either of you like a cup of tea?"

"Yes, please. Thanks," I say, with a smile designed to reassure her that I won't steal her telly while she's gone. Dad gives her a thumbs-up.

Once she's clopped across the parquet flooring to the kitchen, Dad unpacks a couple of wire brushes and starts cleaning the soot from that chunky bit of the boiler above where the flames come up. I don't think I've seen him this energetic in years.

I wander across to the French windows and look out over the long, narrow garden. A graceful lawn curves to the right, ending in a flowerbed at a rear gate. The back of the garden is an odd shape, pinched to accommodate the fact that neighboring gardens must cluster around whatever is past the gate. The tops of all the garden fences form an absolutely straight horizontal line—below it, everything chopped into neat green sections, above it, the clear and empty blue of the sky.

I wish I'd brought my camera. On second thoughts, maybe not. Then she really would think I was casing the joint.

I look over to the left. One house, two house. Vanessa's house. All I can see of it is a sliver of wall, a partial glint of sun off an upstairs window, an angular chunk of roof. It seems very distant from where I'm standing. Silent and separate.

Hey, that must be a record, I hadn't thought about Vanessa for, oooh, half an hour. She snaps back into my head and a stab of emotion starts twitching at my lower lip.

"Please! Young man! You're off the newspaper!" Mrs. Something's standing there with a teacup and saucer in each hand, staring at my shoes.

"Sorry." I hop in a couple of moon-strides over to Dad.

I find I can't drink my tea. I keep turning to look back out of the French windows.

I'm pathetic. I know I am. But I can't help it.

FIFTEEN

second best is better than nothing

On bended knee, I return to the Master. I am clutching at the last straw in the final haystack at the far edge of the world.

Jack brings a pizza round to my house. "Look, I've even got you extra pineapple." I pick a few globs of cheese off the top and unburden my soul. Jack listens patiently to my penitence.

"Told you you'd be back," he says. "Cheer up. You got Kate. I still quite fancy Kate myself, actually. She's a fair piece. If there's not much else on offer, like. Or how about I set you up with Michelle of Ten A?"

"Nooo," I whine.

He sighs. "Listen, I could have swooped in and stolen Vanessa long ago, couldn't I? But I said I wouldn't, and I'm a man of my word, so be grateful. And be grateful James has stayed out of the frame this long. Mind you, I'm not so sure about Vanessa, she's a bit too ice maiden for my tastes. I prefer my women a bit more . . . pleased to see me."

I'm in no mood to argue. Jack is idly nosing through the books on my bookshelf. I'm collapsed on my bed in a heap of self-loathing. Jack keeps shaking his head and tutting.

"Jeez, you're a soppy so-and-so," he says, flicking through a paperback. "Don't you read any proper boys' books? You haven't got a single book about the SWAT team."

"There must be something I can do," I mumble feebly. "I can't give up. I won't give up." After all, I made a vow. There's got to be something.

For a minute or two, there's silence. Jack practices his lollopy cool-walk up and down for a while. Then he plonks himself in the chair by the window and scratches, his legs propped up on the windowsill.

He cranes his neck and smolders at his reflection in the glass. "You're drinking in the Last Chance Saloon, Kev. You're scraping at the bottom of the barrel with your last fingernail, matey."

I raise my head. "I think I've grasped that one, yeah."

"I'm not sure I can let you back on board. After all, you bailed out. You're an unbeliever now. You've hurt my feelings and dissed my methods."

"Oh, belt up! Do you think I'd come crawling back to you if I wasn't at my wits' end? If I'm scraping the barrel, then you're at the bottom of it!"

He raises his hands. "OK, if you're going to be like that, I'll be off."

"Look, I just need . . . a fresh perspective. And none of your management crap. It might be fine for you, but it obviously doesn't work for me. You're the only person I can talk to about this."

Jack breathes deeply and contemplates for a minute or two. "I'm touched, Kev. I really am. I had no idea you could be such a pathetic girlie weed. You are THIS close to blubbing about feelings and relationships, do you realize that?"

I say something unprintable. For a while, there's only the cluk-snik-cluk-snik of the alarm clock on my bedside cabinet.

Finally, Jack steeples a couple of fingers against his lips and frowns. "There is one final strategy that you could use." I sit up, instantly paying attention. "It's not one that's covered in my book, mind. It's too much of a minefield. Not even I have ever dared attempt it."

"Sounds ideal."

"It's the most dangerous strategy you can attempt, one that's normally only employed by girls. Which is why it could—theoretically!—be a powerful weapon in the hands of a male. They don't expect it to be turned against them, you see."

"And it is . . . ?"

Jack drops his feet to the carpet and leans over at me, conspiratorially. "Make her jealous."

I presume my face is registering utter contempt, because he sits back looking disappointed. "She thinks I'm a weirdo," I protest. "She's not going to feel jealous of me, is she? How the hell can that work?"

"Kev, Kev, Kev, you're such a novice in the ways of women. That's not how they think, is it? Jealousy's like a bar of chocolate: they tell everyone they can resist it, but the minute it's dangled in front of them they're like a pack of wild ferrets. And you're in the perfect position. You've got Kate ready on the starting line."

"No," I say decisively. "I'm not treating Kate like that! Anyway, it's too risky."

"Of course, I absolve myself of all responsibility if it goes wrong. This is not something I can officially sanction. But then again, you are turning down your last hope."

He's always been like this. He's the sort who'd start a fight, then stand on the sidelines saying, "Chill, guys, act your age."

"I understand that, but I'm certain," I say. "The answer is no."

"Are you sure?"

"I am completely and totally sure. The answer is no, today, tomorrow and always."

Anyway . . .

Later that night, I ring Kate. "Do you fancy going bowling tomorrow night?"

"Oooh, yes," says Kate. "James and Vanessa are going there tomorrow."

"Oh? . . . Are they? . . . I didn't know." Notice what I did there? I knew all along.

"Yeees," says Kate. "We can all go together."

If there's one thing that I really don't enjoy, it's bowling. I mean, there are things in life that you just HATE—visiting elderly relatives in hospital, having fillings put in your teeth, eating Brussels sprouts, etc., etc.—but there is a whole range of other things, down one level from that, which just sort of make you squirm. Things you want to avoid unless there's absolutely no alternative. Unpleasant things that can turn a perfectly nice day into a vale of tears.

Well, for me, bowling is one of those things. I fail to see what enjoyment anyone can get from it. You roll a cannon-ball across a shiny floor. Then you watch it slide into a gutter. And all the time you're wearing someone else's shoes. Lovely.

The one lucky break is managing to get the lane next to Vanessa and James. The place is very busy, and every other lane is taken. There's the steady BANG-KLANG-CLATTER of balls in gutters on one side, the steady FWEOW-PLIP-PLIP-PLIP of arcade games on the other. That strange bowl-ing alley smell, a mixture of people and wood polish, is duffing up our noses so badly that all we can do is the same as everyone else, and pretend it isn't there.

Kate is wildly enthusiastic. She hasn't stopped talking since I arrived on her doorstep. She made me meet two granddads, an aunt and four cousins—who all live in the same street as her!—before I could drag her away.

James plays it cool. Vanessa more or less ignores me. More or less, but there are a couple of times when I catch her giving me and Kate a funny look.

My God, could it be working?

Kate witters excitedly about Vanessa's commission re: the Pewsey picture for the main hall. Vanessa spent the pre-vious morning capturing the head in front of assorted school buildings, and entertains us with tales of how he can't smile without looking evil. James laughs in all the right places but is clearly still trying to work out what the word "commission" means.

About halfway through, James turns to me when the girls aren't looking. He jerks his head in Vanessa's direction and gives me a thumbs-up. The sewer rat. I give him a tortured smile. Fortunately, Kate inadvertently holds him mesmerized for a while with interesting trivia about bowling, baseball and other U.S.-based games.

While they're discovering a mutual love of sports, I grab the chance to talk to Vanessa. I attempt to be lighthearted and engaging. She fires off a couple of barbed one-liners. I retreat.

And ooooh, guess who gets the highest score of the evening? Ooooh, it's *Jaaayyymzzz*! Oooooh! He jumps up and down with his teeth bared like a chimp in human clothing. And, of course, he then gets a kiss from Vanessa. And one from Kate. And then another one from Kate.

I end the evening with very mixed feelings. It takes a few days to find out via the grapevine where Vanessa and James are off to next. The cinema! New Spielberg film.

My stomach ties itself in knots and then the knots tie themselves in tighter knots. The sewer rat will get her on the back row, in the dark, the place where snogging noises come from.

I call Kate and get her to say no to the party invite she's had for Saturday night. Unfortunately, I have no idea which of the two screenings of the movie Vanessa and James will be going to, so we have to loiter in the thickly carpeted lobby for ninety minutes.

Kate keeps demanding to know why we can't damn well go and get our tickets now. I keep having to buy her things from the refreshments counter to cut off her steady stream of moaning. I tell her I'm very interested in late-twentieth-century-cinema-lobby architecture, and aren't those light fixtures marvelous. After a while, the manager comes over to us and asks nervously why we're loitering. I think he thinks we're terrorists.

The second screening is about to start and Vanessa and James haven't arrived. I've been stood up! Or else they must be coming tomorrow. Kate and I go to the ticket desk. The second screening is sold out.

Kate goes home fuming. Before she goes, she blows a kiss, then sticks one finger up at me and calls me several four-letter names. As she walks away, I shout to her that we'll definitely see the film tomorrow, for sure.

"You bet we damn well will! I'm not standing around in the lobby again!" she squeaks.

"Look, just be on standby, OK?"

Sunday goes much more to plan. Kate arrives grumpily for the first screening, but perks up when she spots Vanessa and James only five minutes later. I cleverly engineer an "accidental" spillage of popcorn in the queue for tickets.

"Oh, I'm so sorry . . . Oh, hi! Are you seeing the Spielberg film too? Really?"

Vanessa gives me that look again. She bounces it back and forth between me and Kate like an Olympic Ping-Pong champion. I definitely get the impression that the plan is working.

James and Kate are oblivious to the whole thing, of course. I've never seen two people get through a giant supersize tub of popcorn so fast in all my life. It's empty before the adverts for the local Indian restaurant have finished.

They spend the rest of the evening trying to suppress burps and giggling. Kate keeps James riveted with interesting trivia about snack foods.

Vanessa has made sure she's sat with James and Kate between us, of course. No chance of conversation, but at least I've short-circuited any risk of her and James exchanging oral fluids. The very thought still makes me feel ill. The film's quite good, though. Kate burbles all the way home. About what, I know not. I grunt here and there and nod in agreement.

I'm more than convinced that the plan is working when, next day at school, I notice Vanessa taking Kate to one side for a chat. Hey, chipmunk-face, hands off my man or I'll scratch yer eyes out! Oh, yeah, you and whose army, Miss Perfect Gorgeous?

No, actually, it's clearly a very civilized chat. Kate laughs a lot. But Vanessa does flash a glance at me here and there. Afterward, I subtly and inconspicuously ask Kate about what was said.

"What was Vanessa saying to you?"

"Nosey!" says Kate, jabbing a finger on the end of my nose. "Aww, is that your cute little insecurities surfacing?"

"No."

The bell goes and a thunderous scraping of chair legs and dragging of feet starts up. "If you must know," says Kate, "she was saying I should watch my step—"

Aha!

"—because she's worried you might be becoming a bit unbalanced. But I told her all the strange things you do are just down to your lovable eccentricity."

"Thanks."

And off she skips to double physics.

With a mixture of careful statistical analysis in the targeting of possible dating venues, plus Kate's enthusiasm for a party, plus classroom gossip, I and my unknowing accomplice manage to cross paths with Vanessa and Sewer Rat no less than eight times in the following few weeks:

One school summer fête; three Sunday afternoons in the park; one school play (evening performance) in the main hall; one meal at the Jade Emperor restaurant; two birthday-related social events (one without the presence of parents). Kate's too busy having a good time to notice my subterfuge, and as an added bonus is too busy having a good time to keep herself welded to my arm like she did before.

At each event, I ensure that Vanessa gets maximum exposure to the idea that she's missing out on me, thereby fanning any flames of jealous passion that may lurk within her heart. The looks she gives me become increasingly smoldering. I sense a crunch point approaching.

How right I am.

It's last thing on a Friday afternoon. Everyone's heading for the bus stop on the main road at slightly less than the speed of sound. I'm taking the corner by the main building at top speed when Kate zooms up out of nowhere and asks for a quiet word.

"What, now?" I gasp.

She nods fervently. We stand in the shelter of the entrance to the modern languages department.

"Oh, Kevin," she sighs. For a moment she seems to be fighting back a tear. Then she blows her nose.

"Oh, Kate?" I say, slightly irritated.

"There's no easy way to say this, so I'll just say it, OK?"

My eyes narrow. "OK."

"I'm afraid . . . Oh, Kevin, I'm so sorry, but . . . but I must let you go."

"Eh? Go where?"

"Go. Be free to pursue other options. Have more time with your family."

I consider carefully for a second or two. "Are you dumping me?"

Kate sniffles into her hanky and keeps her eyes firmly fixed on her shoes. One of them turns inward to point at her other heel. "I've been forced to reconsider your part in our relationship," she says quietly.

Oh, great. How's my plan going to work now? "Why?"

"Oh, Kevin, please try to be strong. I know this is a terrible blow, but I must be true to my innermost feelings. There is . . . another. I love him so much, Kevin, and he loves me, too. Please try to understand, and in time, perhaps, your shattered dreams will—"

"Another who?" I demand.

"James."

"JAMES?" I splutter.

Kate holds on to my shoulders as if I'm about to faint. "It's just that we've spent so much time together recently," she cries. "It's as if destiny has made our paths cross, over and over again. As if fate has delivered us into each other's arms. We've discovered we have so much in common. He's even got a complete set of *Guinness World Records* books too, just like I have. We've come to realize that we belong together, two souls united. Besides, you're hardly ideal boyfriend material, are you? You're grumpy with me, you spend hours examining cinemas, you've never so much as—"

"JAMES?"

She gives me a quick peck on the cheek and hurries away. I emerge from the shadows and watch her skip past the hedges that border the visitors' car park.

Flowing streams of kids are still jostling their way along the paths and walkways. Striding upstream toward me is Vanessa.

The afternoon sun catches her hair, shining into the velvet depths of its darkness. It looks almost blue. She moves like a cat, the momentum of her long steps blowing back the edges of her blazer. She is so beautiful.

"You PIG!" she yells. She stops a couple of meters from me. Suddenly, tears are rushing over her face. She swats at them with her hand. "You did it deliberately, didn't you? You wanted to break us up!"

"No! Please, I—"

"You kept throwing Kate at him, hoping she'd stick, didn't you? You know how naive he is! You used her, you miserable, manipulative pig! Just to break me and James up! What, you can't compete with him on the rugby field so you have to trash his relationships, is that it?"

"NO!"

"Are you going to sour Kate against him now?"

"No! No! It's nothing like that! Please!"

"What is it then? Eh? You tell me! What is it then?"

Her streaming eyes are freezing me. Fire and water together.

"It's . . . because . . ."

I can't speak. I've hurt her. I don't deserve to speak.

"Go to hell, Kevin."

She swings around on her heels and walks away. In the corner of my eye, I catch a glimpse of movement. I turn. Gregory Timms is creeping past nervously, in an exaggerated tiptoe. He looks at me and bites his lip.

"Oo-er," he says quietly.

SIXTEEN

*better to have loved and lost than never
to have loved at all*

Go to hell . . .

. . . Go to hell . . .

So to hell I go.

I can't stop thinking about her. I mean, even more than usual. The memory of a few seconds snipped from the art gallery, the moment when she turns and smiles at me, keeps playing over and over in my head, over and over again, like I can't stop it, all day and all night. And when I know she won't be smiling at me like that again, the empty un-feeling in my chest starts leaping about and slashing at my insides with hot knives.

Jack said it was risky, didn't he? I took the risk, and I blew it. I've hurt the only girl I'll ever love. And she IS the only girl I'll ever love. I know it with a certainty that seems impossible, as if my love for her had been preprogrammed into me, as if my DNA is unfinished without her, as if my every last molecule can never be at peace unless she's here. As if it's destiny.

I spend the whole weekend flat out on my bed, staring at the ceiling. I play music I know she likes, and at first it makes me feel slightly better, almost as if I can be with her in spirit. But pretty soon it gets me down, and Mum starts calling up the stairs to turn that row off and come down and eat your lunch.

I nibble at a plate of pasta. Mum asks chirpily if I want to go clothes shopping this afternoon. I say no. She asks again. I say no. She asks again. I say no. We argue. She goes on her own, departing with a final salvo of hints that she's not going to be able to get anything I like if I won't choose for myself. Dad slumbers droopily in front of Sky Sports One.

Thank God I never brought Vanessa home to meet them. She'd have run screaming. Just as I'd like to. Maybe I should be grateful for the few times I had Vanessa all to myself. Maybe I should be pleased that a background guy like me even got to talk to a shining angel of mercy like her.

Maybe I should go to bed, and go to sleep, and sleep until the pain subsides. Time is a great healer, says the cliché. Maybe I could sleep until I'm three hundred and five and still not wake up free.

I slope off back to my room and try to distract myself by reorganizing the photos stored on my iMac. Fat lot of good that does me. A hefty proportion of my current portfolio includes a certain goddess in earthly form.

It occurs to me that perhaps I ought to delete them. All of them. You know, put the past behind me, all that sort of stuff. Start again, clean slate, look to the future, move on.

Who am I kidding? I know perfectly well that if I hit the Delete key, the first thing I'd do is go scrambling through the depths of the operating system and start running undelete utilities all over the place. I check to make sure that I've actually GOT enough undelete utilities, just in case the madness ever overcomes me at some point.

I call up my all-time favorite photo that I've taken of Vanessa. Aww, come on, don't do this to yourself. You'll only feel worse. You'll only get all miserable and teary.

I click on the Maximize button and it fills the screen. OK, don't say I didn't warn you. I flop back onto my bed, prop myself up on my pillow and stare at the screen.

It's my favorite photo, but even this one can't do her justice. Maybe I just can't capture people's souls the way she can. Something about the colors, something about the amount of background, something about the depth of field.

I keep thinking about our conversation at the gallery, and about her ideas on subject and style. And, all of a sudden, I can see what's wrong. The picture is too much me and not enough her. She was absolutely right. My soft focus, chocolate-box style doesn't suit her any more than it would suit a gorilla.

I load up Photoshop and spend hours fiddling with the color balance and the framing. And when it's RIGHT, when it's HER, suddenly I understand. Because when it's right, it's exactly in the style she would have used. The style that suits her.

I flip back through some of my other stuff, older stuff, and sure enough, all I can see is myself. And my own ideas about what makes a nice image. All very well for cuddly baby portraits, but hardly right for a picture of my true love.

EX–true love.

My favorite photo is now in the stark, journalistic style of all Vanessa's best work. And holy cow, I've caught her perfectly. I've removed the color, and heightened the contrast just a tiny bit. I took it on a small aperture, to hold the focus in the background.

She's looking over her shoulder. Caught in the hey-are-you-taking-a-picture-of-me moment. She's half smiling, half about to speak, framed slightly to the left, cut off at elbow level. Her eyes are bright and dancing, looking right into the lens. Somehow, even in black and white, they're still that melting green. You KNOW those eyes could only be that color.

There's a scattered crowd of kids in the background, none of them looking this way, most of them milling about in the general direction of somewhere-or-other.

Vanessa stands out from them. By her smile, by the slight angle of her head, by being herself.

I lie there looking at the photo for half an hour or so, and then my screen saver kicks in and suddenly I'm looking at Homer Simpson. I joggle the mouse with my foot and she appears again.

It occurs to me that she'll never see this photo. Which is

a shame, because I think she'd like it. Actually, I'm sure she'd like it.

I get up and pull a thin pack of thickly coated inkjet paper from the drawer of my desk. I slot a sheet into the printer and for a few minutes it hums and whirrs away, spitting out a copy of the image, line by line.

She can't mind if I just give her the photo, can she? Even if she's boiling mad at me?

SEVENTEEN

nothing can go wrong this time

Apparently, she does mind. Well, no, to be strictly accurate, I don't get the chance to find out. The photo spends most of the week tucked away in my locker, eight lockers down the row of lockers from her locker.

She's barely speaking to me. A muffled "Hi" is the most I get. And in that "Hi" she's clearly saying: Look, we have to be in the same class together, so let's keep our distance and get on with it, OK?

She's busy with photos of her own. She comes into school on the Monday with her fresh-from-the-printer's commissioned picture of Mr. Pewsey rolled up and wrapped tightly in plastic under her arm. It's all a big secret until the unveiling on Thursday.

It's the last week of term. The twelfth graders have all finished their exams and are going to pieces like a detonating chicken. After Friday comes the summer.

I can't live with this guilt until September. I have to do something. I have to give her the photo, just to tell her that I'm not a monster and that I never meant to hurt her. Whether she believes me or not.

Monday goes by, Tuesday, Wednesday . . . I can't simply walk up to her and hand it over and say sorry. It seems so feeble. I can't give her MORE than the photo, like a huge bouquet or a sports car or something, because then I'd look like a creep. I can't make NO attempt at apology, because then I'd look like the gutter slug she currently thinks I am.

Wednesday . . . Thursday . . .

Tomorrow is the last day of term. My innards are twisted by a feeling of time running out. I reason to myself thusly: If I can't simply GIVE her the photo, I'm going to have to get it delivered to her in some way. I can't ask a third party to deliver it for me: (a) because I can't risk her thinking I'm a wimp for not bringing it myself, not on top of everything else, and (b) because there's nobody I could trust with it, not even Jack. Quite apart from the fact that I've totally lost faith in him as a relationships strategist, he'd undoubtedly start embellishing whatever I told him to say. Out of kindness to me, I'm sure, but he wouldn't create the right impression.

So, anyway, that option's out. I can't send Vanessa the photo in the post, either. Hardly a meaningful gesture, that, is it? Here's a photo that captures the very essence of your soul, to humbly apologize for everything I've done, and I do hope the post office haven't lost it, crumpled it or sent it to Brazil by mistake.

Could I e-mail it to her? Here's an electronic file to humbly apologize for . . . No. Doesn't sound right. Anyway, the original file's enormous, it'd take half an hour to squeeze down the phone, AND she'd have to use her own photo paper to print it out. Mind you, she did get some for her birthday . . . No. Forget it.

Could I take it to her house while I know she's out? Would I be able to get to the front door without her dad hitting me in the face, or her mum calling the police?

In the end, and with time ticking away here, I decide that the only thing I can do is leave it for her where I know she'll find it. It's a ropey compromise, but it'll have to do. I can't go slipping it into her schoolbag, that's a sure road to Disasterville if ever there was one. I COULD pin it to her locker . . .

Of course, the difficulty with that is: how to do it without anyone seeing. If someone sees me, my cover is blown. I might as well stand up and announce my feelings to the entire school. The Warwick High Chinese Whispers Society would have her believing I'd skipped across the sports field with a big heart chalked on the back of my blazer or something.

No, it's a private thing. It must be done privately. I must at all costs avoid causing her further embarrassment.

I could come in tomorrow very early? Nope, teachers rise from their tombs and walk the corridors at sunrise. Plus, Vanessa might turn up early by chance and catch me.

And then the solution smacks me around the face like a wet haddock. Thursday at five p.m.—"Inspirational, Atmospheric Public Art in Schools. In association with the Arts

121

Funding Foundation of . . ." blah, blah, blah. There are announcements on orange photocopy paper pinned to every notice board from the canteen to the cricket pavilion. At five, everyone who's anyone left on school premises will be in the lobby of the main hall watching Vanessa's picture of Pewsey get unveiled. Including Vanessa. It's absolutely guaranteed that she won't see me deliver my photo. And very little chance of anyone else seeing me either! Of course, it'll mean missing Vanessa's moment of triumph, but I don't think she'll be missing me, so apart from that . . .

. . . it's perfect.

It's more than perfect, it's fate. The universal karma of life itself is telling me that it's a brilliant idea. Events have placed themselves so exactly that nothing can possibly go wrong.

It's almost five. I've done my homework in the library and with a casual glance at the library's clock, I shove my books back in my bag and head out into the dust-drenched afternoon sun. Nobody is about.

I walk between the giant, silent cubes of the art block and the admin block. The whole school is quiet, and the tiny squeak of my shoes seems deafening. At this time of day, at this time of year, places look like they're made out of kiddies' building bricks, all square and slapped down anywhere there's space. Something to do with the angle of the light, and the sweatiness of the air. It's kind of unreal, like I'm walking through a film set, and every structure is hollow and propped up inside. Reddish-yellow light holds itself in poses of shapes and shades.

I walk past the back of the canteen. Once all the foodie business of the day is complete, Fat Lunch Lady and Thin

Lunch Lady usually sit around smoking and drinking sherry. The emergency exit door is propped open to let the fumes out, and then let the two of them out once they're ready to crawl home.

I walk through the main building. The door to Mr. Pewsey's office is ajar. I catch a faint odor of cough syrup and unhappiness.

The long corridor, lined with lockers, is a perfect tunnel of straight lines all heading for convergence at a vanishing point somewhere over by the bike shelters. It's an art teacher's dream, full of rigid perspective and neatly shaded areas. I pass the buckled-in locker at the end of the row, the one that appears not to have been touched since about 1972. I retrieve the photo from my own locker, along with the blob of Blu-Tac adhesive that's been stuck to the roof of it for a term and a half, and step back along the line to Vanessa's.

I stick the photo, tucked into a brown envelope, to her locker door. I give it a good press, to make sure it doesn't fall off overnight. Not much of a romantic gesture, just leaving her a blob of Blu-Tac.

I look at it for a moment or two. I'm still undecided about this last bit. Oh, what the hell, yeah, it'll make things clearer. I pull out a pen and write "I'm sorry" across the bottom right corner of the envelope.

Then I go home. I spend half the night in a restless daze, worrying if I've done the right thing. Nothing went wrong, did it? That's what I'm worried about!

EIGHTEEN

vanessa in the sky with diamonds

I oversleep. Before I'm awake, I keep hearing this distant voice . . . a high voice . . . Mum's voice . . . calling up the
stairs . . . and then . . . shouting up the stairs . . . and then . . .
OH MY GOD IT'S TWENTY TO NINE!

When I come running through the school gates, the first
thing I see is Miss Gretchen, queen of the boilersuit, standing guard at the double doors to the main hall. And I mean
standing guard. She's not just milling about waiting to
pounce on kids who've forgotten their PE gear. She's standing there, arms folded, flat-top hairdo bristling, barring entry.

I haven't got time to worry about that now.

I hurtle into the classroom with seconds to spare. I collapse at my desk, panting hoarsely. Nobody takes the slightest notice. They're all too busy either collecting around Kate to console her (the girls), or collecting around Sewer Rat to brood silently and read car magazines (the boys).

Eh? I tuck in the back of my shirt, and straighten my tie, and wipe the sweat off my forehead with the sleeve of my blazer, and wonder what the hell is going on today.

Enlightenment comes in the form of Gregory Timms. He sits down at the desk behind me and starts brum-brum-ing his car-shaped eraser up and down the windowsill.

"There was an envelope stuck to Vanessa's locker first thing this morning. Everyone says it was a love letter from James, because he wishes he hadn't dumped her for Kate. It had 'I'm sorry' on it."

Oh God almighty, for—That's a thought, where IS Vanessa?

"Kate's ready to kill him," continues Gregory. "James says he doesn't know anything about it. But then he would, wouldn't he? Kate smacked him over the head with her French textbook just before you came in."

Waitwaitwait! Hang on! Go back a bit.

"What's Vanessa got to say about all this? Where IS Vanessa?"

Gregory bites his lip. "Didn't you hear? She's in deep doo-doo," he says, his mouth movements much louder than his voice.

For a second, he's got me thinking of farmyards, but then the truth spears me through the head.

125

"W-WHAT?"

"Pewsey went ape at her. She was distraught, said she'd done her best, but he wouldn't listen. They were all there: staff, governors, her parents, the mayor, some creaky old photographer from the *Evening Herald* . . . Pewsey said she'd insulted him personally."

WHAT?

With her photo of him? Her commission? Her passport-to-greater-things project? I think my brain's turned sour, I can't take this in.

"But . . . how . . . ?" I stammer.

"None of us in here has seen it," shrugs Gregory. "Queen of the boilersuit's keeping people away while they take it down. Maybe Vanessa printed his eyes on back to front or something."

There's a violent scraping of desk legs from the back of the classroom. James is banging things around to cover up the fact that his eyes are going all watery. "When I find out who set me up, I'll kill him!" he grunts.

Kate emits a shriek of disdain from inside her cocoon of female friends. The cocoon glares at James and he slams another chair down. I feel like jumping up and shouting, "Nobody's set you up, you dozy great twit, that photo was from me!" But a vaguely troubling something in the phrase "I'll kill him" stops me.

I want to scream. I want to hide.

There's the regular end-of-term assembly of the entire school at nine o'clock. Our usual route into the main hall takes us right through the lobby and right past Vanessa's commissioned photo.

By chance I'm one of the first to arrive. The caretaker

and Miss Gretchen have lifted the paint-marked dust cover that's been draped over the photo and appear to be in conversation about it.

When they hear us coming, they hurriedly get it covered up in a matter of seconds. But not before I've had a clear look at it.

It's the photo Vanessa took in the canteen on her very first day. The one that first made me realize she's into photography too. The one of Pewsey, standing with his tray, having his suede shoes mopped by Thin Lunch Lady.

It's printed tall and narrow, about two meters high. It's cropped at precisely the right place, with Pewsey's back to the far right of the frame, and the head of the mop poking out at the bottom left, hardly noticeable at first. The look on Pewsey's face is half embarrassed, half defiant.

And it's EXACTLY right. Vanessa's eye for these things just takes my breath away. This is EXACTLY the atmosphere of the school, in one image: standing tall, with a so-what attitude, and slightly shabby around the edges. It's funny, and it's honest, and it's true.

And then it's gone. The smeary dust sheet gets wrapped back around it, hanging like a curtain in a sad and tatty theater. The caretaker mumbles to Miss Gretchen about fetching his tool kit to unscrew the picture from the wall. There's a brass plaque on the far side of it. The line of kids bustles too fast, and I don't get time to read it.

Everybody shuffles into the main hall. There's that last-minute atmosphere of hey-we're-getting-outta-here-today. Some of the younger kids start toting two-finger guns.

I'm slap in the middle of a sea of bobbing heads, next to

Jack. He's just whispered something to Claire of 10D and she's moved up a couple of seats.

"Silly cow doesn't know what she's missing," he grumbles. "Anyway, Kev, I bring a disappointing news update from the James front! He's still saying it wasn't him."

"Maybe it wasn't," I say quietly.

"Naaah, it was him all right. It's the only explanation that makes sense. He's in denial, you see. He's blanked it from his brain. He's gone totally off the path of correct girlfriend management and it's confused his tiny little mind."

The staff begin taking their seats on the stage. The caretaker's had to borrow some extra chairs from the canteen to fit them all in. The loud murmur reduces to a low murmur as Mr. Pewsey fights his way out from behind the pulled-back stage curtain and trudges to the front of the seated rows of teachers.

There is silence as he finishes chewing on one of his pills. He sighs and slips the bottle back into his top pocket. He speaks slowly, deliberately, painfully.

"Today . . . is the last day of the school year. And instead of my usual good-humored address to you all, today I find myself preoccupied with the consequences of modern society's decline. I do not relish any occasion upon which I am forced to reprimand a pupil, and I relish even less those occasions upon which I am forced to reprimand a pupil because they have made a personal affront against me."

He slaps his lips together in slow motion and gazes around the hall. There is silence. I can feel my heart, thudding cold and fast.

"It is the last day of the school year, and I am forced to draw your attention to the conduct of Vanessa Wishart of

Ten L," says Mr. Pewsey. "She was given a position of trust and responsibility, and she has abused that trust. She was asked to produce a work to reflect the school, and instead has produced one which mocks and derides it. The shambles of yesterday afternoon's unveiling is an occasion upon which I do not wish to dwell."

He runs a hand over the pocket with his pills in.

"As you know, ladies and gentlemen, I am the most forgiving and liberal of head teachers. But I will not put up with this form of brutalism. Wishart of Ten L must stand as an example to you all. That is why I have to disrupt and taint our final assembly with such tedious business."

Silence.

"The moral fiber of the student body of Warwick High has been found wanting once too often. The lack of respect far too many of you exhibit on a daily basis has now influenced a once-promising pupil." He delicately smoothes the top of his head. "I have not yet made my decision as to what form of action is appropriate, but whatever my decision turns out to be, it can be taken by all of you as but a small warning. Let's see how many such warnings it takes before you improve your attitude, shall we? That is all."

No . . .

The noise level rises. Pewsey turns away, staff begin to stand, kids wriggle in their seats, looking at each other blankly, not really caring, counting the minutes till the end of the day.

No!

They can't do this! HE can't do this!

Something erupts in my head. That gaping feeling that comes with bad news or sudden horrors or knowing you're sitting on the-one-roller-coaster-too-far.

But it's too late. Pewsey's gone, the staff are filing out of sight, kids are traipsing back to classrooms in meandering streams, taking their time, making the journey last, delaying lesson one.

I slouch along with them. But it's like I'm sealed off. Vacuum-packed. Only I can see the terrible injustice of it all. Am I the ONLY ONE HERE WHO CAN SEE THE TERRIBLE INJUSTICE OF IT ALL?

And, as soon as that thought has faded away, I find I'm not making my way to history with the others. Jack's shouting something, but I'm not listening. I can't hear the rest of them, or see the rest of them. I'm on my way to Pewsey's office.

Wooaah! No, you're not! Whaddya think you're doing?

I walk and walk and walk. I AM going to talk to Pewsey! No I'm not, yes I am, no I'm not. I weave my way around the buildings, walk, walk, walk . . .

I hear the bell go for the end of lesson one. Walk, walk, walk, keep walking, through the crowds, through the corridors. Whaddya think you're doing?

That gaping feeling inside hasn't gone away. I keep thinking about Vanessa.

And somehow, I draw strength from her. From her confidence, her abilities, her way of looking at the world.

Here's the new me.

I knock confidently on the door of Pewsey's office. Luckily, his secretary's on her tea break, otherwise I'd have been wrestled to the floor and forced to make a proper appointment.

His voice moans painfully from inside. "Oh, for heaven's sake, what is it NOW?"

I go in, straight in, straight ahead, right up to his desk.

"Watts?" he says, screwing up his eyes as if a squinty look at me will make things clearer.

"I need to speak to you, sir."

"Wonderful. Make a proper appointment with my secretary."

"I'm sorry. It can't wait, sir."

"Watts, unless the school is burning down or there has been a major civil emergency on the High Street, I'm afraid it will have to wait. I am busy."

"I'm really sorry, sir, but it can't. It's about—"

"Unless I'm badly mistaken, you have in fact been familiar with the words 'I,' 'am' and 'busy' since year one, haven't you?"

"It's about Vanessa Wishart, sir."

He blinks at me vacantly for a second. "Is it indeed?"

"Please don't be angry with her. It isn't fair."

His fingertips sit delicately on the blotting pad in front of him. He frowns. "I beg your pardon?"

"Punishing her is wrong. I don't mean to be rude, but it's wrong. That photo is a work of art."

He's sitting so still you can tell he's on the point of exploding. "That photo, Watts, is an embarrassment to this school."

"But we should be proud of it. It's brilliant. It stands out. It's totally original. It shows the school exactly as it is. Not as results, or buildings, but as it is for those of us who actually form it. This commission is very important to Vanessa, sir, and if it's important to her, then it's important to me. I know she wouldn't have done anything to deliberately upset anyone."

131

"She betrayed the trust placed in her."

"Sir, please, all she's been is honest, and true to herself."

He's so still there's only the hostility in his eyes to remind me he's still alive. "Say one more word, Watts, and you'll be in trouble as well."

"How about if I said I'D chosen the photo, sir? Or swapped it for the one she really wanted to use, as a practical joke? Or—"

Mr. Pewsey scrambles for his pills and crams one between his teeth. "Enough! Fine, have it your way! Take a seat in the corridor outside. I'll be speaking to you as soon as my next meeting is over." He twitches his head at me, like a bird eyeing an insect in the grass. "Why, boy? Why should something like that be so important to you?"

I think he's genuinely puzzled. Here's the new me.

"Why?" I say quietly. "Because I love her. I love her with all my heart, and with all my soul. And even if she doesn't love me back, I'm a better person for knowing her. I owe her everything."

Silence. For a split second, I think Pewsey's going to burst out laughing. I hear the slight creak of a floorboard behind me.

I turn. Standing in the doorway are Vanessa and her parents. Frozen, staring at me. Her mum holds a handbag motionless, against her chest. She lets out a high-pitched choking noise.

"Good God, it's that idiot boy," growls her dad.

NINETEEN

amen

Two hours later, I'm still perched on one of the viciously uncomfortable comfy chairs outside Mr. Pewsey's office. Vanessa and her parents came out half an hour after I did. Not at quite the same speed, though. I avoid looking at them, the same way you avoid people you know but don't want to talk to in shops.

And now I'm sitting here waiting for Pewsey's summons. A couple of teachers have come and gone. Mr. Arbuthnott's in there now. Pewsey ushered him in with a "Oh, very well, come in, this had better not take—"

Clunk. Door shuts.

I think both my buttocks have gone numb. The bell went for break time a couple of minutes ago. I stare out of the wide bank of windows across the corridor from where I'm sitting. The trees that border this side of the playing field are shuffling gently in a breeze I can't feel. Harsh sunlight spikes through the windows, making hot trapezoids on the linoleum. I can smell the school, that peculiar institutional smell that you stop noticing after a while. It makes me feel like the new kid again, tiny and alone, wanting to go home.

I watch people walk across the window's view from left to right, from right to left, from left to right. Going somewhere. Doing something. Jack appears, catching up with a small group of girls. He takes Claire from 10D to one side. Her friends stop and watch from a distance. He says something to her, his arms wide in broad, open-palmed gestures. Claire and her friends walk off. After a minute or two, Jack shrugs and lollops out of sight.

I go back to wondering what's happening in Mr. Pewsey's office. Then footsteps approach down the corridor. Half a class-worth of shoes and socks and trouser legs clatter by, trailing snips of conversations. And then it's quiet again, dust clouding in the sunlight.

I sigh and flop back in the chair. Suddenly, I notice that someone has sat down next to me.

Vanessa.

We look at each other in silence for a second.

"Looks like we're both in trouble, huh?" she says quietly.

"Yup," I say, nodding. I find I can't meet her gaze anymore, and start examining my fingernails instead.

"I talked to Kate and James. To set them right on a couple of points."

"Uh-huh?" I croak. Gosh, those nails could do with a cut. Must remember.

Long, yawning, huge, gigantic silence.

"I was, umm, surprised at everything you said in there."

"Uh-huh?" I croak very quickly.

"But . . . It made a lot of things suddenly fall into place. It explains a lot."

"Look, the photo on your locker. I'm sorry about—"

"I knew it was from you," she says. "I knew as soon as I saw it. The only people in this school who could take a picture like that are you and me. And I'm in it. Let's face it, James wouldn't know a camera from a camper van, would he?"

I let out a long, slow breath. "I didn't mean to cause more trouble. I just thought you'd like it."

"I do. I like it very much. Not that, you know, I make a habit of admiring pictures of myself, but you know what I mean."

"I know what you mean." I smile at my fingernails.

"It's not like anything you've done before," she says quietly. "It made me think. Made me realize certain things about you. Why did you do it in that style?"

I shrug my shoulders and pull a quick aww-heck-I-dunno face. "Because that's the real you. The way you are . . . the way I like you."

"I like you the way you are too."

My head does a lightning ninety-degree turn and I look into her face again.

"You were just you."

"I'm just me now," I whisper. "Honest."

"I know," she whispers.

She takes my face in her hands. Her wonderful eyes remove my doubt, my fears, my uncertainty. Spectacular eyes.

And she kisses me. Those soft and tender lips against mine.

And my heart is mended.

And I'm looking forward to the summer.

About the Author

Simon Cheshire is the author of several popular books for young readers published in the United Kingdom. He also writes and presents *Fast Foreword,* a bluffer's guide to literature, on Oneword Radio and is constantly fiddling about with his Web site at http://uk.geocities.com/simoncheshireuk.

He writes in a tiny little office that used to be a closet, where he'd be helpless without his books, his Apple Mac and a regular supply of chocolate. Most of his best ideas come to him while he's asleep or staring out of the window. He lives in Warwick, England, but spends most of his time in the world of the strange and unusual.